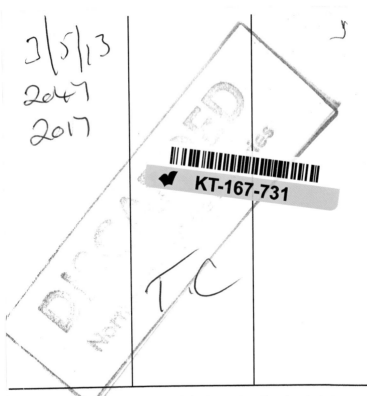

Please return/renew this item by the last date shown. Books may also be renewed by telephoning, writing to or calling in at any of our libraries or on the internet.

Kill Slaughter

When a California train is robbed of $30,000, and two Pinkerton detectives killed, bounty hunter James Slaughter rides to investigate. But a cloud of fear hangs over the railroad town of Visalia and even the judge is running scared.

Beaten up, jailed and framed by the sheriff's deputies, Slaughter survives assassination attempts but is hit by more trouble as vicious range war erupts on the prairie. With his stallion and his sidekick having more fun than he is, can he trust fiery bar girl, Anna Matiz? And with the body count spiralling, can the bounty hunter claim the missing cash and even find himself a loving woman?

© Henry Remington 2012
First published in Great Britain 2012

ISBN 978-0-7090-9818-8

Robert Hale Limited
Clerkenwell House
Clerkenwell Green
London EC1R 0HT

www.halebooks.com

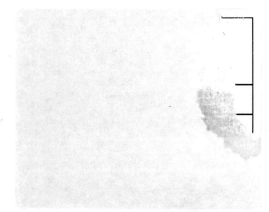

Typeset by
Derek Doyle & Associates, Shaw Heath
Printed and bound in Great Britain by
CPI Antony Rowe, Chippenham and Eastbourne

Kill Slaughter

Henry Remington

A Black Horse Western

ROBERT HALE · LONDON

ONE

The distant sound of the locomotive's pistons pumping, the sight of black woodsmoke being forced in a gasping stream from its tall stack as it climbed the grade of the mountainside, made three figures who had been lurking in the shade of an ancient oak skulk out into the harsh noon sun of Southern California. For reasons known only to themselves they were garbed in the white sheet robes of the Ku Klux Klan, the slits of the pointed hoods revealing only their eyes and the holes of their mouths.

'Here she comes,' a husky-voiced one rasped out. 'Dead on time.'

Another thumbed back the hammers of a twelve gauge double-barrel shotgun. 'Dead they will be if they give us trouble.'

All three had gunbelts slung around the waists of their costumes, revolvers in the holsters on their hips. The third one appeared slimmer and shorter in stature than the other two and the voice was that of a youth, higher in tone and tremulous. 'He said there was to be no killing unless—'

'He's not here, is he?' the first man replied. He gasped with effort as he used a stout oak branch as a lever to complete the twisting of the single-track rails away from the ties. 'We're the ones in the line of fire.'

The chuffing of the locomotive grew louder and louder. The gradient had slowed it to about twenty miles an hour. The three would-be robbers had piled up rocks on the track behind them. They faced it, weapons ready, watching the oncoming cowcatcher, the smokestack billowing out its black clouds and behind that the window-holes of the cab.

The engineer poked a goggled head and shoulder out of the cab, his left hand on the handle of the steambrake valve. 'Hell's teeth!' he cried to his fireman as he spotted the ghostly figures through his steamed-up goggles and hauled at the valve handle. 'Who are these jokers?'

The stoker could hardly hear him because of the boiler roar, but yelped, 'What's wrong?'

They were both soon to find out as they heard the steel wheels scream and the locomotive screech to a crawl. But it had not slowed enough, hitting the broken rails at five miles an hour and tipping as if in slow motion off the track. Hot steam spurted over the stoker but the sound of his screams was drowned by the thunderous noise as the engine ploughed down the rubble of of the embankment.

The engineer jumped for safety, or so he hoped, cartwheeling out of the cab to crack his spine and head across a rock and lie supine as the two passenger cabs behind jerked to a sudden halt; people and their bags were tossed about like dice in a gambler's cup.

The locomotive had come to a halt, its stack twisted, nose buried in the rubble. The rest of the train was still on the track, including the iron-clad baggage car which was the focus of the 'klansmen's' attentions. They stood, tensed, hearing the agonized screams of the fireman, his face and body red-scalded, the shouts of passengers trying to right themselves, and the wheezing of the loco-motive as if it was gasping its last.

The leader of the robbers went jumping down to take a look. Blood trickled from the engineer's mouth. He was stone cold dead. A shot reverberated as the robber put his revolver to the forehead of the fireman and blasted a hole through his head.

'I can't abide that screaming,' he gasped out as he climbed back up to the track. 'Put the poor devil out of his misery. Come on.'

He led them at a jog-trot past the carriages, guns at the ready in case any passenger should be foolhardy enough to take a pot-shot. They climbed up to the rein-forced luggage van.

'Open up,' their leader shouted, poking his long-bar-relled .45 through a small, barred window-hole. 'Toss your guns through the window first. Then step out with your hands high.'

'No way, mister,' the guard shouted from inside. 'You think I'd trust you?'

'We don't want to hurt you. All we want is what's in the safe. So get it opened up.'

The youngest of the trio was still at the side of the track, revolver in fist, looking back in case of trouble. Some of the passengers, men, women and children, were climbing out of the wreckage, stumbling about. The young one fired a shot over their heads and strode back towards them, shouting, 'Stay where you are.'

There had been no reply from the man inside, so the leader growled out, 'We've got dynamite. We'll blow the caboose to kingdom come unless you get out here double quick. Don't get me angry,

The second robber was standing behind him, his shotgun raised. 'Let me give him a blast with this.'

The leader held up his hand to quieten him. Sure enough there was the sound of a key in the lock, the strongroom door was opened and a little man in the uniform of the Southern Pacific Railroad, California Division, appeared, the look of a startled rabbit in his watery eyes as the revolver barrel was thrust into his Adam's apple. 'Right, get back inside. You done what I said?'

'I ain't arguing, mister,' the guard whined.'That's it.'

Sure enough the safe door was swinging wide. He was pushed aside as both men took a look. 'Good,' one muttered, as he pulled out bags of gold coin, stacks of greenbacks. 'Looks like our information was spot on.'

His accomplice held a gunny sack wide as the leader packed the loot into it. 'That's about it,' he said, peeling a $20 note from one of the wads, and studying it against the light. 'Looks like the real McCoy. Here, pal.' He stuffed it into the guard's vest. 'That's for your help.'

'What about the mail?' his companion asked. 'Those packets look important.'

'Stick 'em in the sack if you want. But we've got enough. My friend, you know how much this lot is worth?

We're damn well rich.'

They scrambled out, after locking the guard inside his cab, and tossed the key into the weeds. Then they strode back to where the youngest one had the bruised and battered passengers lined up against the train and was demanding they toss their valuables into another gunny sack. Children were snivelling, hanging to the legs of their parents, terrified by the sinister appearance of the hooded robbers with their slits of eyes.

'Come on,' the leader shouted. 'This lot don't look like they're worth robbing. Let's get out of here.'

But at that moment a passenger appeared at a door of the train, a thickset man, a revolver in his grip and blazing lead.

The sawn-off exploded into the air as its possessor was hurtled back by a bullet hitting him like a sledgehammer. The leader of the robbers raised his .45, crashed out a shot and kept on firing until their assailant tumbled out of the door and landed on his back. Blood was pumping from his chest as he gasped his last breath.

'There always has to be one, doesn't there?' The husky-voiced man spun on the others. 'Anybody else want to try me?'

'Frank's bleeding bad,' the youngest one called out, kneeling beside the fallen robber. Blood was reddening the white robe. 'It's his shoulder. What we gonna do?'

'Shut your mouth, you fool. No names I told you. Go get the horses.' The speaker glanced at the mob of startled passengers, and as the black powder smoke curdled about them he turned his revolver on his fallen comrade, as if in half a mind to dispatch him. But he obviously had

9

a change of heart. When the young one galloped up, leading two mustangs, he growled out. 'Help me get him on his horse.'

Frank, whoever he was, managed with their help to climb into his saddle, swaying as he hung to the saddle horn. The leader slung the two tied-together gunny sacks across the shoulders of his own mount, fired his last shot over the heads of the crowd and spurred away.

The crowd of passengers watched him go, followed by the youngest one in flowing robes, leading the mustang of the gun-shot outlaw. Soon they were gone, riding away beyond the dark oak.

'What we gonna do now?' a woman shrilled, looking around them at the empty expanse of wilderness.

'Nothing we can do except wait,' a farmer said. 'Wait for the next train along from Visalia in five or six hours.'

'Jeez,' a small boy cooed. 'That was exciting! Is the man dead?'

'You stupid boy, of course he is.' His mother clipped him about the ear. 'There's nothing exciting about this.'

'Look at all that blood,' a woman moaned. 'Never knew a man had so much blood.'

Shouts from along at the caboose distracted the passengers who waddled away along the track like a chattering gaggle of geese to see what had happened.

A ferrety-faced individual furtively stayed behind. The besuited corpse looked like some sort of businessman. Maybe. . . ? He snatched away the gold watch and chain, and stuffed it in his pocket, along with his gold wedding ring and his wallet. A card on the front of this last indicated an all-seeing eye, the insignia of Chicago Pinkerton detective agency operative. Ferret-face removed the bills from inside and tucked it back in the stiff's pocket. 'It ain't gonna be no good to him now,' he excused himself, and hurried away to join the crowd. 'More fool him. He shoulda got himself a proper job.'

TWO

Six months later – the mountains, twenty miles south of Tucson, Arizona.

A rider drew in his stallion on a ridge and tugged his hat down over his brow to shield his eyes from the setting sun. He gazed across a boulder-strewn valley to a narrow defile in the low hills on the far side. There was no sign of them. Just the deadening silence of the desert. No sign of life, but for a golden eagle, spiralling, searching, as he was for his prey. He guessed they were headed for the border. What spoor there was on the rock hard ground had led him this far. He needed to catch up with them before darkness enclosed them. Before the Apache got them. Or him.

The rider himself had the looks of an Indian. His thick black hair hung down beneath his hat, his dark face was deeply grooved, eroded like the mountains themselves. His body was lithe, with powerful shoulders beneath a torn leather topcoat. His cotton pants were tucked into moccasin boots. But he was no Apache. In

12

fact, James Slaughter was a quarter-breed Comanche on his mother's side. His grandmother, a German Protestant girl, had been with a covered-wagon party of pilgrims wiped out by a war party as they headed west. His grand-daddy, the Comanche buck, had raped her and, for some reason, left her alive. From Slaughter's point of view that had been kind of him.

He nudged the stallion down the slope and let him weave his own way across the valley as two men hidden in the rocks on either side of the dry gulch watched. One saw the sun's glint on the tin star pinned to his home-weave shirt and aimed the sights of his single-shot Enfield rifle on it. But the ambusher decided to wait until the rider got closer.

'Pa-dang!' The bullet screamed past Slaughter's ear as he entered the gully, whistling away, chiselling rocks.

Simultaneously another rifle shot clapped out from the opposite side of the low cliff sides, making his stallion leap to one side as if a rattler was lunging his fangs at him. It was as well that he did, for the bullet ploughed into the spot where they had been a second before.

Slaughter leapt from the saddle, snatched his Spencer carbine from the boot, slapped the stallion's rump to send him careering on along the gully, and rolled into the cover of the rocks.

'We sure been dry-gulched,' he muttered, as he wrig-gled higher up the cliff. 'I walked right into it. What's the matter with me?' He ducked down as two more blue screamers tore across the top of his hidey-hole. 'I ain't gonna be gettin' much older if I don't watch out.'

The would-be bushwhackers were two murdering

drifters who had stove in the head of Tucson's Polish pawnbroker, stolen his silver, raped his wife and slit her throat. Slaughter had trailed them since dawn.

'Hey, Sheriff,' one yelled from up above, his words echoing away on the wind. 'Where are you? Come out and fight like a man. I allus wanted to kill a lawman.'

Damn fools, he thought, as he raised himself to a crouch and peered around. Why didn't they try when I was out in the open and they had the chance? 'Throw down your guns, boys,' he yelled back. 'We'll give you two shithouse rats a fair trial 'fore we hang you.'

This only produced shrill laughter, a shower of obscenities and another two shots that bounced over his head. It was obvious that they had single-shots and had to pause to reload. So he took the opportunity to climb as fast as he could for the rim, which was more of a jumble of huge rocks tumbled together in some volcanic eruption aeons ago.

Another bullet sought him as he reached the top, winging past as he leapt away, the moccasins finding secure purchase as he bounded from one rock to the next until he judged that he was above the man on his side.

Slaughter levered a slug into the breech of his seven-shot. He was in luck. He looked across the ravine and saw one of his assailants silhouetted against the blood-red sky. Their gaze met simultaneously across the fifty-yard gap. Both squeezed their triggers. Two shots clapped out. There was silence for a moment. Then the murderer clutched his gut and tumbled down into the gulch.

'Hell, Jake! What—?' the second fugitive's voice rang

out with alarm, helping Slaughter to place him. They were the last words he spoke,

'Hi,' Slaughter called, as he stood above him. The man spun with surprise, fired wildly. The Spencer's slug hit him between the eyes and he back-dived off the edge to join Jake below.

'Gotcha!' Slaughter said, with some satisfaction, although it would not bring back the Pole with the unpronounceable name, or his poor wife.

He bounded down to the two bodies sprawled in their death sleep, made the sign of the cross over them and growled, 'Rest in peace, fellas.' Then he put two fingers to his lips and gave a piercing whistle.

Soon the stallion came galloping back along the ravine, swirled to a halt, and nudged Slaughter hard in the chest with his proud Roman nose which was a sign of Andalusian lineage.

'Hiya, Henry. OK, don't git pushy. Here y'are.' He pulled a couple of sugar lumps from his pocket and pressed them into the horse's mouth. 'Mission accomplished, huh? We done well, more by luck than judgement once again. But it looks like we gotta camp out with these two bozos tonight, if you don't object to their company.'

A young, neatly-dressed stranger was seated in Slaughter's armchair in the shade of the overhang outside his office when the sheriff rode down Tuscon's wide main street the next morning, the two corpses slung over their horses behind him.

'You waiting for me?' he grunted, as he ditched the

15

bodies on the raised sidewalk beside him.

'Yes. I see you've been busy.' The young man rose to his feet and offered his hand. 'William Pinkerton. My father founded the agency. I'm working out of our Kansas branch.'

'Howdy.' Slaughter examined the Enfield P53. 'British army issue for their troops fighting a losing battle out in Afghanistan. We imported a million of 'em for our li'l shindig. Old percussion-cap muzzle-loader. Not my style. These two shoulda updated their armoury. They mighta had a chance.'

'Really? You may remember the robbery of a train in California six months ago? It was bringing a consignment of five thousand dollars in gold coin, plus brand new greenbacks, twenty-five thousand dollars' worth, for the use of the National Bank here.'

'Sure, I heard about it.' Slaughter nodded. 'Any luck?'

'No, that's why I'm here to report our lack of progress to the bank directors, unfortunately.'

'You'd be due a good slice of the cash if you got it back?'

'Exactly, but all of our leads have fizzled out in the Californian dust. One of our operatives got killed in a shoot-out at the scene. Another was nosing around in the Visalia area and seemed to be getting somewhere.'

'So?' Slaughter raised a querying eyebrow. Pinkerton took a cardboard note from his pocket.

'They found him strung from a telegraph pole alongside the line. This was pinned to his chest. "You send any more of your nosy Chicago detectives thisaway – this is what they get".'

'Charming.' Slaughter's grooved face split into a grin.

'A Pinkerton man's life ain't all honey, huh?'

'Exactly. Actually, we are hard-pushed. Bigger fish to fry. We're closing in on the Cole Younger–James brothers' gang in tandem with the Federal secret service.'

'Bigger reward, huh?'

Young Pinkerton ignored the remark and followed Slaughter into his office, offering a cigar from his leather case.

'Thanks.' Slaughter took a bottle of bourbon from his drawer, filled a glass. 'You wanna snort?'

'Too early for me.'

'Yeah, me, too.' Slaughter slumped in his padded swivel-chair and put his heels on his desk, raising the glass with a sigh of bliss. 'So, whadda ya want?'

'I've heard about you, Mr Slaughter. You've got quite a reputation as a fast gun and thief-catcher. I hear you served as an officer with General Forrest during the recent unfortunate disagreement between the states.'

'That what you call it?' Slaughter gave a caustic cackle. 'Yeah, only made Loo-tenant. Guess I don't like taking orders.'

'And afterwards you fought for three years with Juárez in Mexico against the French.'

'Two. When Juárez put that Austrian fop, so-called Emperor Maximillian up against a firing squad and the Frenchies scuttled like rats from a sinking ship, Benito paid me off. Services no longer needed. So I came home.'

'Yes, so now you're Tucson's sheriff. Are you paid well?'

'Hundred a month. It ain't so bad, although the town's filling with roughnecks now the railroad has

17

arrived. Gamblers and whoremongers are moving in. There'll be trouble.'

'Quite.' William took a box of Bryant & May's phosphorus matches from his suit and lit their cigars. 'I could double that. We need a man like you to investigate the Visalia robbery.'

'Yuh?' Slaughter sucked at the green cigar with obvious appreciation. He blew a smoke ring. 'That's hardly worth me gettin' out of this comfortable chair fer. To tell the truth, my friend, I'm sick of killers and killing. I've had too many years of it. I'm looking to make a big slice of dough so I can buy myself a piece of land, breed horses and maybe my own kind if I can find a suitable piece of muslin who feels the same way.'

'You mean raise a family, Mr Slaughter? A very sound idea. OK. Should you recover most or part of the stolen cash, bring the fugitives to justice, not only is there a five-hundred-dollar reward on each man offered by the bank and railroad company, jointly, you would also be due a tenth of the recovered monies.'

Slaughter pondered this as he refilled his glass. 'I doubt if there's any cash left after six months. It'll have been blown.'

'No, it doesn't seem so. We have very few reports of any of the notes being passed. We have all the serial numbers of the bills. It seems to me like the gang is hanging on to it for some reason.'

'Yeah? You sure you don't want a drink?' The sheriff raised his glass. 'Here's to the Reverend Elijah Craig.'

'Who's he?'

'Preacher in Bourbon County, Kentucky in 1789 when

he invented this nectar of the gods.' Slaughter grinned and tossed it back. But his expression changed when the door was shoved open and a corpulent man in a bowler hat charged in, shouting,

'Slaughter, this has got to stop.'

'What has?' growled Slaughter.

'This. Those corpses outside. Ain't you never heard of bringing a man in alive? Me and the town council are trying to impose some law and order on this town. This does not set a good example.'

'Meet our mouldy mayor,' Slaughter jeered, the bourbon souring him. 'No need to tell you he's a lawyer. He'd like to spin his hocus pocus defending those sewer rats and make himself a few cents.'

'It's just not right. A sheriff needs to temper justice with mercy. You're more of a killer than them killers. You don't give 'em a chance,' the mayor blustered.

'What chance did they give the pawnbroker and his missus? You ever find a bullet in their *backs* you let me know. They had their chance. Seems like most killers prefer a fight than to be brought back for a hempen necktie.'

The mayor's face had gone as scarlet as his mottled nose. 'Don't give me that guff. You're answerable to the council.'

'Here.' Slaughter unpinned his sheriff's star and tossed it to the mayor. 'Pin it on your arse. But don't prick yourself. You might go bang and let out all that hot air. I resign.'

'Now, James,' the mayor wheedled. 'I'm only . . . it's not too much to ask.'

Slaughter rose agilely to his feet and stretched, making the mayor flinch. 'Piss off, you fat turd.'

When the mayor had bustled off Slaughter grinned at Pinkerton.

'So when do I start?'

'Just as soon as you're ready. Perhaps you'd like to step along to my hotel and sign the contract?'

'You got one ready? That means you expected me to agree.'

'I like to be prepared. My father taught me that.'

'Very wise.' Slaughter relit the cigar and handed the box of matches back. 'You oughta be careful with these. I read that some Italian princess accidentally stepped on one and set her dress alight. Perished in the blaze. You just never know what's gonna hit ya outa the blue. Of course, I don't suppose you wear a dress in private life.'

'You're an amusing man, Lieutenant. Would you be interested in joining us permanently?'

'Nah, there ain't no such thing as permanent. All I want's my ten per cent. Then I'm out. This is my last job. Then I start looking for my ranch.'

Slaughter stuffed his sparse belongings: a worn toothbrush, spare pair of woollen socks, marlin spike, baccy, and a box of a dozen bullets in his warbag, chucked the jail keys on the desk, grabbed his Spencer and slung the canvas sack over his shoulder. He sauntered across to the spacious Alhambra saloon, but there was no sign of his runty little sidekick, Aaron Snipe.

'Maybe's he's down at Rosita's bordello,' the 'keep suggested.

'More'n likely.' It was the dirtiest, noisiest, smelliest, lowdown joint in town. Yes, Aaron was there, clamped in the capacious arms and balloonlike bosom of a Mexican whore, doing a dainty two-step around the hard-mud floor.

'Hi, Lootenant,' Aaron whined in his saw-twanging Deep South drawl and swayed to a halt. 'Meet Ephiginia. Ah thank ahm in lurve agin!' He shoved the lady towards Slaughter who had found a barrel to sit on against the adobe wall. 'She's all your'n.'

Ephiginia squawked as she landed on Slaughter's lap. Her expanse of flesh in the skimpy dress spread over him like warm milk. Her garlic halitosis and heavy stench was too much. He opened his legs and let her crash to the floor.

'Ain't you indulging?' Snipe asked.

'I'll pass. Where were you when I needed your assistance yesterday morning?'

'Aw, I'd got one hung on from the night before. Didn't seem no point in slowin' down.'

Ephiginia's screams of indignation had added to the din in the adobe sinbin. Her scarlet sisters, Dolores, a skinny scarecrow, and Lolita, a toothless painted crone, were trying to haul her to her feet, but they all collapsed amid shrieks of laughter.

'Have a drink, Lootenant.' Snipe proferred a goatskin of mescal. 'Best cactus juice. Sorry I missed cha.'

'Thass OK. I solved that problem,' Slaughter raised the skin, catching a jet of the murky liquid in his mouth. 'Called in to tell ya I'm catching the midnight train to Yuma, then on up to Bakersfield. Just thought

I'd say so long.'

'Hail!' Snipe was wearing the torn, tight butternut suit he'd worn when he joined Forrest's regiment in Memphis, Tennessee. Home-woven, it was much the worse for wear, but still more or less intact. Crammed down on his bony head was the grey forage cap they'd issued him with all those years before. 'Whatcha goin' there fer?'

'The Pinkerton agency has landed a federal contract to track down a bunch of California train robbers. Seems like they ain't got time so they've farmed it out to me. It gives me authority to act on behalf of the government, for what that's worth.'

'But what about your job here?' Snipe's Southern drawl screeched like an out-of-tune fiddle. 'You was doin' purty well.'

'The mayor objected to me not bringing prisoners in on the hoof. I told him where to stick his badge. Nah.' Slaughter waved away another offer of the goatskin. 'That stuff'll send you crazy.' He got to his feet. 'I'm gonna git me some grub.'

'Wait a minute, you leathery ol' bastard,' Snipe slurred, trying to hang on to Ephiginia at the same time. 'If you're off to California you must be sniffing big bucks.'

'Not really,' Slaughter lied. 'If you wanna side me I can manage thirty a month outa mine. There could be trouble. Seems like the fellas in a town called Visalia don't take kindly to strangers nosing around.'

'Oh, yeah?' That was a red rag to a bull to the wiry little Snipe. 'We'll soon see about that.'

'If you're coming I'll be loading Henry on to the freight train at eleven thirty tonight. Don't be late.'

THREE

Their journey took them through Fort Yuma to Bakersfield, then north until, halfway along the sixty-mile stretch to Visalia, the locomotive halted by prior arrangement for them to unload their horses. They watched it rattle on its way. This was the spot where the derailment and murderous robbery had occurred.

'Surprising what the flash of a Pinkerton badge can do,' Slaughter remarked as they took a look around. 'It'll even stop a train for ya.'

'Here's where the engine went off the rails,' Aaron cried.

'Yup. That's purty obvious. And when they'd robbed the train they headed south? Nope, that was just a ruse. They circled north-west towards the big lake. That's where we're going.'

'Ain't any of the notes been cashed?' Aaron asked, as they had headed off in that direction.

'Yup. A twenty-dollar bill. The train guard's doing two years in San Quentin for being in on the robbery. At his trial he hotly denied it, said one of the *bandidos* just gave it him as they departed. I'm inclined to believe that.'

'Ain't no others been passed?'

'Only one that young Pinkerton knows of. A woman of indeterminate years and profession cashed a fifty in the Puebla de Los Angeles, a one-horse town over on the west coast. She claimed some gambling man pressed it upon her. Couldn't remember what he looked like 'cause it was dark at the time.'

'That's a helluva lot of cash to give a whore.'

'Seems like she's more a high-class hooker who specializes in the gentry. A blonde, in her forties or even fifties, but still a good-looker. She claimed the guy had a big win in the casino. She got off.'

'So, what do you think, James?'

'All these little details add up.'

They travelled at a fast lope most of the day until they spied Tulare Lake spread out like a sparkling small sea.

They followed the wooded shoreline until they heard voices and saw a collection of ramshackle cabins. On the wall of one a deer's hide was nailed out to dry, a bloody buck's head, a six-pronger, was ensconced on a tree stump and his carcass hung from a bough. It was seething with flies. A gang of tangle-haired Indians wandered about or squatted lethargically in the dust.

There were dead critters everywhere: a rack of geese and ducks yet to be plucked; a row of otters; beaver pelts, as stiff as boards, were piled on a wagon; and one of the Indian squaws was chewing at a doeskin to make it supple.

'No wonder they lose their teeth young,' Slaughter muttered. 'Just what goes on here?'

25

'Looks like a place of rest and recreation for weary hunters,' Aaron opined. 'Shall we go in?'

The main cabin bore the sign, BOATS FOR HIRE. There was a makeshift jetty where a few punts and row-boats bobbed. Out beyond stretched the sun-sparkling waters beneath a clear blue sky of the great Tulare Lake, which was some fifty miles long by thirty wide. In fact, you couldn't see the other side.

'No, I'm going in alone. You stay hidden in case of trouble. There's something shifty-looking about this place.'

'Jeez, Loo-tenant,'Aaron moaned. 'I got a terrible thirst. And my belly's rumbling, too. Smell that cooking.'

'I don't want folks to know there's two of us. From here on we're on our own. We need our wits about us or we could end up dead. So hang on here.'

There was indeed an appetizing scent coming from a big clay oven outside the main cabin, which an Indian woman was feeding. In this mild climate who needed an oven indoors? Slaughter rode in, hitched the stallion to a rail and stepped through an open door of the dilapi-dated cabin. A bunch of men in the room fell silent, casting hostile looks. A corpulent man with a ruddy, moon-round face was behind a makeshift bar of a couple of planks rested on barrels.

'Howdy, gents,' Slaughter cheerfully greeted them, pulling off his riding-gloves. 'What kind of pizen's that ye're supping?'

'Corn whiskey, my own brew,' Moonface muttered, reaching for a chipped mug and filling it from a barrel propped on the bar. 'Quarter a shot.'

Slaughter hitched aside his big Schofield six-gun, dug in his pocket and slapped down a few coins.

'Correct.' Moonface tossed them in a drawer. 'That'll put hairs on your chest.'

'You don't say?' When he sampled it Slaughter collapsed with a fit of coughing, spluttering out the moonshine, gasping as he recovered. 'Jeez, it's got a kick like a mule.'

'He can't take your whiskey, Elijah,' one of the men jeered, as the others' sullen looks broke into cackles of merriment at his discomfiture.

'I can take it.' Slaughter blinked tears from his eyes and took a more cautious sip. 'I can take any liquor anybody throws at me from Colorado to south Mexico.'

At least it had broken the ice and he began to pass the time of day with the congregation. Some were attired like hunters in peaked caps and plaid coats, goose-guns by their sides. Others, in floppy-brimmed hats and dirt-engrained clothes, had a more ruffian air.

'How about a couple of thick steaks from that horned critter you got hung outside?'

'Sure.' The barkeep nodded to an Indian woman who shuffled away to tend to the barbecuing. 'That's a dollar.'

'You sure ain't cheap.'

'Who's done all the work, the slaughterin' and guttin'?' Elijah moaned. 'Me.'

'Oh, I thought maybe them Injins outside did it for you.'

'Them lazy devils?' Elijah scoffed. 'They ain't much good to anyone. I pay a couple of 'em fifteen dollars a month to do a bit. Then all their damn relatives and kids turn up to eat me outa house and home.'

'Tough.'

After a while the hunters had departed and only the surly no-goods hung around in the cabin bar. 'What brings you this way, mister?' Moonface asked.

'Let's speak frankly.' Slaughter lowered his voice, tipping him a wink. 'I'm a friend of them three who robbed the train six months back. Wanna locate 'em. Got a job lined up might interest 'em.'

Moonface Elijah gave a scoffing laugh. 'You hear that, boys? This bozo reckons he's a pal of them train robbers.'

'Oh, yeah?' jeered one of the whiskey sots. 'Sounds more like you're after a share of that thirty thousand dollars they lifted.'

'Hear tell they passed through here shortly afterwards,' Slaughter pressed. This was according to the information given by the Pinkerton agent before they hanged him high. 'You must remember that.'

'I got a bad memory,' chubby Elijah whined. 'Cain't even remember what I did yesterday.'

'Come off it,' Slaughter growled. 'The guy was gunshot in the shoulder. That ain't something you forget.'

'Maybe it ain't wise to remember too much around these parts,' one of the men butted in, threateningly. 'Or ask too many questions.'

Slaughter eyed them aggressively but the group glowered back. 'Ain't gettin' nowhere here. Where do I eat? Outside?'

'Sure,' Elijah whined. 'Then I'd advise you to be on your way.'

'You would, would you?' Slaughter replied. 'And I'd advise you to be more polite to a paying customer.'

He stepped outside to sit on a fallen tree trunk as the Indian woman served him platters of juicy venison slices with corn bread.

'Great!' Slaughter grinned as he looked over at the trees and gave a wave, although there was no sign of his friend. 'His nostrils will be twitching,' he muttered, 'and his mouth watering watching me git stuck into this.'

He glanced at the defeated-looking bunch of Indians as he chomped his grub. Modocs, he guessed. They'd had the stuffing kicked out of them for centuries by the Spaniards. Captain Jack had made one brave last stand five years ago and been hanged for his pains.

Fat, bossy men were a particular irritant to James Slaughter. Always had been. And when Moonface bustled out to see how he was doing, he carefully laid the platter aside and growled, 'My compliments to the lady. A very good cook. But, if you ask me, *you* could do with a sizzling.'

'What?' the barman exclaimed. 'Get your hands off me.'

But it was too late to protest. Slaughter had grabbed him around the waist and hoisted him up to sit on the stove. 'Don't remember nuthin', don't ye?'

The moonface screamed and struggled, legs kicking, as Slaughter held him on the hot oven. 'What'll it be? Medium rare or well-cooked?'

As Elijah bawled and his pants scorched the men from the cabin tumbled out to gawp, but seemed no threat, just cackling at the 'keep's discomfort. 'How's your memory now, pal?'

'All right,' Moonface screamed. 'I'll tell you.'

Slaughter dumped him down as Moonface hopped about flapping at his sizzling trousers, making the men jeer the more. 'There was three of 'em,' he screeched. 'But I don't know who they was. They plugged the man's wound and went on their way.'

'You ain't cooked enough. Your arse needs another five minutes.' Slaughter grabbed him but the barkeep screamed, falling on the ground, howling, 'Go on, kill me. I don't care. *They*'ll kill me iffen I say any more.'

'It's true.' One of the down-and-outs intervened, pointing an ancient rifle at him and the others skulked, reaching for pistols in their belts. 'His life wouldn't be worth living.'

Slaughter abandoned the barman, his hand snaking towards the grip of his Schofield but knowing he was out-gunned. Could he take them all? Suddenly a flock of pigeons burst noisily from the trees and the men looked askance.

'Maybe he ain't alone,' one said.

'You half-wits wanna find out?' Slaughter growled.

'It ain't nuthin to do with us,' the spokesman whined. 'All I'm telling you is the ones you're looking for ain't so far away. So you go make mincemeat of them, not us.'

Slaughter smiled, grimly, nodded at them and turned to swing on to his stallion. 'Good day, gents,' he called, as he clipped away. 'Nice to have made your acquaintance.'

He headed away along the lake and as he rode Aaron came galloping out of the brush. 'I was ready,' he shouted. 'We could have taken 'em.'

'I ain't here to kill small fry. It's the ones at the top I want. They've told me enough to know I'm on the right track.'

'True,' Aaron agreed. 'Could have been a nasty blood-bath.'

'Here.' Slaughter pulled a greasy steak from the pocket of his leather jacket and chucked it at him. 'Eat your supper. I'll tell you somethang; even *you* couldn't have swallowed that booze.'

FOUR

'Not only have you been snoring all night like a flatulent warthog,' Slaughter said, 'but you stink worse than your hoss.'

'Darn my socks, Loo-tenant,' Snipe whined. 'Ain't no need to come out with the insults this early in the marnin'.'

'Yeah, I bet they do need darning. I bet you need to scrape 'em off with a knife. When's the last time you had a bath?'

'A bath?' Snipe looked startled. 'Why, last Christmas. You know that.'

'No, I don't know that. Maybe it was the Christmas afore.'

They had spent the night in a cove of rocks on the lake's western shore. Now the sun was rising in the east, casting a golden pathway across its waters. Slaughter had fed their fire to boil up his battered coffee pot. He cast his tin mug aside and unbuckled his gunbelt, tossing it on to the sand. He pulled off his calico shirt to stretch his rippling-muscled torso, discarded his moccasin boots and cotton pants and stood in a pair of soft perforated doeskin shorts ideal for riding. Or swimming.

'Looks like Christmas has come early this year, Aaron.'

'Aw, no, you go ahead. Not me, Loo-tenant. My mammy allus said too much bathing weakens a man. I could catch my death of cold.'

'That suit you're wearing is caked with mud and almost in tatters. It's time to toss it on the fire. Get it off, Corporal. I hate to think what your lice-ridden drawers are like. Git them off, too.'

'No way. You gawn plumb crazy, James?' Snipe began backing away, scrambling to his feet, seeking escape, but Slaughter dived on him, wrestling him to the ground, hauling off his boots, trousers, and filthy long johns as Aaron kicked and struggled.

Slaughter hauled him to a sitting position. tore off his ancient jacket, shirt and tattered undervest, got his skinny, white *compadre* in a necklock, hoisted him up and dragged him to the water.

The naked Snipe screamed with shock and tried to splash away, but Slaughter wasn't done yet, producing a bar of carbolic soap, giving the shivering little man a hard rub over, then put a hand on his head and thrust him under. Snipe spluttered, spitting out a small fish as he came up. 'Aagh!'

'Thar y'are. Reckon you're done.' His former lieutenant gave a howl of mirth, snorting and splashing and scrubbing himself. When he came out he reached for a carpetbag he had hanging from his saddle horn and tipped out its contents. 'A few thangs I picked up in Bakersfield when we changed trains.'

'You had this all planned.' Snipe sat huddled, shivering, trying to dry himself with his old clothes. 'It ain't right.'

'Clean pair of combinations.' Slaughter tossed them at him. 'Get 'em on. Socks. Shirt. And' – he imitated a trumpet sound – 'Ta-ra! A new suit.'

'Oh, no! Do ya know how long my mammy took making mine, dying it yaller with walnut juice? I cain't throw it away.'

Slaughter emptied the old one's pockets, held it aloft, fastidiously, and dropped it on the flames. 'Look at them fleas leapin' for their lives! Put on your nice new striped one, Aaron. And here, the *pièce de résistance*, a new hat.'

Aaron peered at the bowler that Slaughter punched into shape, and howled, 'I cain't wear that. I'll look like a pox doctor's clerk.'

'That's just what ye're gonna be, Mister Snipe. How did you guess? It's your disguise.' From the bag he produced a number of bottles. 'Aniseed for bellyaches. Oil of earthworms for bruised bones. Belladonna for muscle spasms. And several bottles of cough medicine. It's a mix of camphorated opium and cannabis. Very popular. The apothecary explained them all to me.'

'What'n hail I want with them?' Aaron was reluctantly pulling on his new clothes.

'Ye're gonna hawk 'em around the town of Visalia. A travelling salesman yo're gonna be. If you run out of lotion you can easily dig up a few more worms. You're my underground agent from now on. Ain't ya pleased?'

'Huh!' Aaron pulled on his old boots. 'Don't see like I got no say in it.'

'We're nearly at the north end of the lake. You're gonna ride back east until you hit the railroad and go into town before me. I'll be in in a day or so. You gotta act like you don't know me. Put your gun in the bag. You don't know how to handle thangs like that.'

'So where you going?'

'I'm heading on north. According to the map there's a big rancho run by one of the old-style dons. I plan on paying 'em a call.' Slaughter was back in his own clothes now, flicking his damp hair out of his eyes and going to collect his stallion. 'Come on, what ya waitin' fer? Oh, here y'are. Seven dollars fifty. Your first week's wages. Book yourself into a hotel room. And start selling them bottles. And, Aaron,' he pointed a finger at him, 'stay off the booze.'

Wildfowl were so plentiful on the lake he could have potted a goose with his pistol. The water, too, was full of fish as the way an osprey came zooming down to snatch fat ones with his claws demonstrated. As Slaughter headed away from the *laguna*, settling the stallion into a long high lope, riding deep in the saddle, it was evident that these rolling grasslands were richer than anything he had seen in the south. The light green *alfilleria* was cropped not only by cattle but by numerous herds of wild antelope mingling with them.

However, as he rode past one of the stands of low-hanging, gnarled oak he suddenly was confronted by a big grizzly that stood up ten feet high on his hind legs to view him. Beneath him was the bloody carcass of a fawn he had captured. The big bear sniffed the air as

Slaughter veered away, then charged on all fours without warning.

'Giddap!' Slaughter kicked his heels into the stallion and slapped his haunch, sending him sprinting. For moments the grizzly was a match for them, hurtling towards them at a good thirty miles an hour, but the startled horse outpaced him and after fifty yards the bear gave up the race, standing to give a mighty roar of anger.

'Guess he didn't like having his breakfast interrupted.' He slowed the stallion's gallop and patted his neck. 'Lucky for us you've got a tidy acceleration, eh, boy?'

Across such magnificent parkland he rode for most of the morning, the stallion eating up the miles, without encountering another human. But suddenly a band of horsemen appeared on a rise, rifles and lances held in their hands, gave shrill, warlike shrieks and sped down en masse towards him. Another man might have drawn his gun and given them battle, or turned tail and fled, but Slaughter knew that that would be futile. He pulled his horse in and faced them.

They kept on whooping and screaming until they were almost upon him, then swirled their mustangs to surround him. They wore the high-crowned sombreros and range leathers of *vaqueros*, sitting their horses to grin and jeer at him.

'Why do you trespass on our land?' their leader, on a fine white Arab mare, demanded in Spanish.

He was a young man of more elegant appearance than the others, flashily attired in silver-embroidered black velveteens. His saddle horn was solid gold as, it seemed, were the big spurs on his boots. His sombrero had fallen back to reveal a thick mass of black hair. He would have been handsome but for his front teeth which were crossed into each other and gave his high-cheekboned face a wolfish air.

'Nobody told me it was your land,' Slaughter replied in the same lingo.

'Where are you from?'

'Down south.' Confronted by the tasty mare Henry was getting mighty frisky and he had a job to control him. 'Tucson way.'

'So, what are you doing here?'

'Jest passin' through,' Slaughter drawled in English. 'Ain't doin' you no harm.'

'Is that so? Maybe you are planning on rustling some of our beeves. You look the type.' The young Mexican also spoke in English, but strongly accented. 'We hang rustlers around here.'

'I might look like a saddlebum, but I can assure you I ain't after your cows. Looks can be mighty deceptive, you know.'

'So, where the hell are you going to?'

'I was heading for Visalia. Must have lost my way. So, who are you, pal?'

'Pal?' The Mexican gave a mocking laugh as he, too, tried to control his mare which was getting uppity. 'I am no pal of yours. I don't like the look of you, stranger. But I like the look of your horse. Maybe we should talk further.'

'Maybe we should—' Slaughter tried to shy aside as a rope came spinning out, dropped neatly over his head and tightened sharply around his shoulders, almost jerking him from the saddle. 'Hey!'

'Bring him,' the young man cried. 'Take his guns.'

'This ain't very civil,' Slaughter protested, but was unable to prevent the grinning *vaqueros* from disarming him.

'Now you are just a toothless wolf. We can do as we like with you. What are you, an Indian? Nobody would object if we killed an Indian.'

'Well, I am and I ain't. Three-quarters white man on my mother's side. Must admit to havin' a Comanche grand-daddy.'

'A 'breed? Worse than a damn Indian.' One of the *vaqueros* had leaned over to frisk their captive and produced the Pinkerton pass from the pocket of his leather coat. He tossed it to his chief. 'What have we here? So you've come to spy on us, Agent James Slaughter.'

'That's me, *amigo*. So what's *your* handle?'

'Ricardo de Estudillo Puyol.' The young man drew himself up, proudly. 'My father owns all this land – the Laguna Ranch – as far as you can see. Forty thousand acres of it.'

'So that's huccome you can afford the fancy saddle? Daddy provides for you.'

Ricardo scowled at him. 'He may be interested to question you, 'breed. Come.' He jerked his mare roughly around. 'Bring him.'

The stallion had no hesitation in chasing after them, even if Slaughter wondered, as they all went charging off, whether this had been such a good idea.

Except for a central tower block the ranch-house was a

single-storey adobe building. It was three-sided around a central courtyard, stables with off to one side, a farrier's, corrals and the *vaqueros'* bunkhouse. There were peach, grape, and orange orchards watered by sparkling streams. The outward-facing walls had iron-barred windows or gun-slits to ward off attack. The Indian servants were housed in what looked like a chicken shack.

It being the hottest time of day the start of the siesta, an air of lassitude reigned over the place, that is until the *vaqueros* came charging in. One, named Mino, still had hold of his lariat, pinning Slaughter's upper arms, and he gave it a vicious jerk, pulling him out of his saddle.

Slaughter, however, landed with catlike agility on the balls of his feet, caught hold of the rope and pulled Mino, too, from his mustang. The *vaquero* tumbled awkwardly and the lieutenant helped him on his way with a right cross to the jaw that sent him rolling in the dust.

Slaughter loosened the rawhide rope and tossed it away from him as a low-necked coach was driven in. There was a finely dressed young lady in the back – her hair the colour of sun-ripened corn – accompanied by her stern-faced duenna.

'Well, whadda ya know?' Slaughter murmured, meeting her blue eyes. 'Maybe it was worth the ride after all.'

The girl gave a sharp scream, almost a warning, as behind him Mino climbed to his feet and sped at him, a knife in his hand. The American spun round, parried the blow with his right arm, kneed the *vicioso* in the groin. As he doubled up, Slaughter hit him with a left fist like iron, pounding home two more jaw-crunching blows in fast succession.

'Has that settled your hash, or you want more?' Slaughter asked, stamping on the man's wrist and kicking the knife away.

'Enough of this nonsense,' Ricardo shouted. 'The *Americano* is a guest in my father's house.'

Amid the *vaqueros*' jeering laughter, Mino lay in the dust, feeling his jaw. 'This is not over,' he hissed. 'One day I will keel you.'

'You can try.' Slaughter gave a shrug and turned away to get an eyeful of the blonde-haired *señorita* who, in a rustle of satin skirts, was stepping from the carriage showing a shapely, silk-stockinged ankle. He gave an exagerrated bow, offering his hand to help her descend. 'Pleased to meetcha, your ladyship.'

He met her eyes, huge, blue pools that he suddenly wanted to drown in, but she frowned angrily, trying to detach her slim fingers from his grip. 'Maybe we can get closer acquainted while I'm here?'

'How dare you?' she cried in Spanish, pushing him away. 'Who is this person, Ricardo?'

'He calls himself Slaughter. Do you want me to soften him up for you, sis?'

'*Sí*, his arrogance could certainly do with being taken down a peg or two.' She brushed past him and went into the house as her duenna flicked her fan at him and bustled after her. Ricardo laughed and jumped from his mare, which a groom led away.

'I will introduce you to my father,' the young Mexican said. 'I am beginning to like you, *Americano*.'

40

'What about my hoss?' Slaughter grabbed hold of the stallion to restrain him, for he seemed eager to follow the mare. 'Henry takes after me when it comes to the ladies. We cain't help ourselves. But I don't want him wearing hisself out.'

'That is something we can discuss. I will have them kept apart for the time being.'

'Yeah, well make sure they're well apart or he's likely to kick up one hell of a commotion.'

Don Miguel de Estudillo Puyol had much the same looks as his son, but his thick mane of hair was streaked with silver, his dark face grooved by lines of age. And he had a far more sombre expression.

He presided at the dinner table in a curious chair made of longhorns' horns, with a stuffed leather seat and back. He wore a crisp white shirt, a cravat, loosely tied, and a silver-buckled belt holding up his velveteen pants.

'So, you are a Pinkerton investigator?' he remarked as he sampled a glass of musky red wine and indicated that the bottles should be passed round. 'I should warn you, the previous one met a grisly end.'

'So I heard.' Slaughter took a swig from his filled glass. 'I was planning on keeping my identity secret but Ricardo here has rudely announced it to one and all.'

'We suspected him of being a rustler. You must admit he has the ruffianly looks of one.'

'Ach, we are plagued with them,' Don Miguel growled, in his gravelly voice. 'Not so long ago before the *Americanos* came to this country it was the most pleasant, peaceful spot in God's kingdom. Since '48 everything has gone to the dogs. Mexico ceded California to your government, so then came tax collectors and sheriffs and lawyers. There was no crime before you came, no need for prisons. We dealt with any arguments in our own way. First there was the gold rush and then the railroads brought eastern scarums flocking in, and farmers moving in on our land.' He shrugged his shoulders with an air of resignation. 'What can we do but try to fight them off?'

This big room where they dined was an odd mixture of poverty and luxury. Earthen, not wooden, floors were covered with oriental carpets. At one end were Don Miguel's four-poster bed and ornate desk, at this end the long table. Around the table were a collection of cousins and aunts, poor relations, Slaughter judged, by the way they ignored the conversation and concentrated on filling their bellies. The food was the usual fare of chilli con carne with corn cakes, but plenty of it, and in the centre were bowls of fruit from the orchards.

Slaughter's attention, however, was drawn to Raquel de Estudillo Puyol, who had changed into yet another emerald satin dress after her siesta, her magnificent cascade of blonde hair pinned back by diamond-encrusted combs. Indeed, he found it difficult to keep his glance from the V-shaped dip of her dress from which her breasts, as pale as the pink-tinged petals of the first magnolia blossom, appeared eager to tumble from her bodice. At least it seemed so in his imagination. It was almost as if she had dressed – or undressed – to tempt him.

'Father sees himself as an old bull,' she explained,

'dragged down on all sides by the wolves.'

'So I am,' Don Miguel growled, 'and I might add, by the luxury-loving ways of my son and daughter.'

'Nonsense,'she cried, giving Slaughter a dazzling smile. 'Would you expect me to ride into town on a *burro?*'

'It would do you no harm once in a while. As for Ricardo, he seems to think I have pots of gold coin hidden here, there and everywhere.'

His son showed his crossed fangs in a devilish grin. 'Well, haven't you? Anyhow, you should see the stranger's stallion. A magnificent beast. I wish to make use of him with my mare. So I have invited Slaughter to stay a few days.'

'Waal, I dunno about that,' their guest drawled. 'Where I come from we generally git a stud fee. For Henry the going rate's a hundred dollars.'

'A hundred!' Ricardo shouted. 'You're crazy.'

'OK, seein' as you folks are providing me with such generous hospitality I'll make that a cut-price offer of fifty.'

'We are not robbers,' Don Miguel put in. 'Of course we will pay for the stallion's services.'

'Good. In that case,' Slaughter eyed the young lady's bosom again, 'me an' Henry will regard this as a li'l holiday.'

'Let's go out to look at the sunset,' Raquel suggested, after the meal. 'It's such a beautiful night.'

'One sunset is the same as another,' Don Miguel grumbled, but he slowly, helped by a servant, followed along, a box of fat Maduros cigars under his arm and

Ricardo brought a bottle of port. They took seats in basket chairs on the porch and looked out across the courtyard to the mountains silhouetted against a crimson western sky.

'Waal, you sure ain't done too bad for yourselves,' Slaughter drawled, as he sucked at a cigar and took a quaff of his glass of port. 'Yes, sir.'

'*Sí*, but for how much longer?' Don Miguel remarked. 'We are being robbed on all sides by you Yankees.'

'I ain't a Yankee. I fought the damn bluebellies for four years.'

'I mean those men in Visalia summoning me to appear in court. They have the nerve to claim I have no legal right to this land. I have the parchment deeds granted by the King of Spain to my ancestors a century ago. But they try to tell me they are null and void.'

'You don't say.'

'I do say.'

'Yeah, but who would you say is stirring thangs up? Who's behind this?'

'Why, there's two of them in cahoots. The American rancher, Henderson, and his slimy lawyer lickspittle, Bogbinder. The sheriff is in their pay. They won't be happy until they are in possession of my land and we are thrown out, homeless and destitute.'

'Oh, Father,' Raquel cried. 'Surely you're exaggerating.'

'You will see, my fine lady. It is happening everywhere. Throughout the state the Mexican landowners are being outrageously cheated of their fortunes.'

'But, Father, none of us would have fortunes if the

44

Americans hadn't flocked in,' Ricardo put in. 'Before '49 you used to butcher steers simply to sell their hides. Suddenly you saw the value in meat and sold the beef at inflated prices to the gold miners. The railroad has brought us prosperity, too. You can't deny that.'

'Pah!' Don Miguel growled, struggling to his feet. 'You may enjoy this cool mountain breeze but not me. It chills my bones. I'm turning in.'

An Indian woman helped him back into the house as Ricardo said, 'The Old Man lives in the past. He is not the man he was since a fall from his horse.'

His hearing seemed first class, however, for Don Miguel stuck his head out of the door and roared, 'Yes, and you can't wait for me to be dead.'

Raquel smiled and said, 'Shall we stretch our legs and go look at this fabled stallion of yours?'

'Sure.' Slaughter strolled away with her, but Ricardo caught up, a bucket of barley in his hands. 'This will give him energy for tomorrow.'

Slaughter leaned on the corral rail and fed his horse a handful. 'You can put that dangling dong of yourn away,' he said with a grin. 'You ain't needing it just yet.'

Raquel laughed, pushing the American away with a finger on his chest, for he had cosied up kinda close to her. 'The same goes for you, *señor*.'

'Don't let him make any improper advances, sister,' Ricardo called, as he went off to attend to his mare.

'What other advances would an *Americano* make?' she scoffed.

'I noticed a lot of bars on the windows. Do you Mexicans still lock up your daughters?'

'No, but my father uses other methods on over-excited suitors. He shotguns them in the *cojones*.'

'You're a very outspoken young lady.' Slaughter winced, but coiled an arm around her and pulled her into him. Her lips were soft, warm and sensuous as she allowed the kiss – indeed, responded willingly.

Over in the courtyard a *vaquero* was strumming a guitar as others lounged around him, one breaking in with snatches of song, others taking him up in chorus, rising and falling, languorously. A big Spanish moon was rising high and Slaughter murmured, 'Seems like a night made for love.'

Raquel's cheek dimpled, mischievously, as she pulled away. 'Don't count your chickens before they're hatched, gringo.'

'Not so fast.' He caught hold of her tight up against the corral fence, jerked undone the bowstring of her bodice and dipped a hand inside to pull free her pale breasts. 'These look very kissable.'

'No!' She broke from his grasp, trying to cover herself. Her eyes blazed like a tree'd mountain cat's. 'Do you want me to scream?'

'Maybe that ain't a good idea.' He stuck his thumbs in his gunbelt, took a deep breath and drawled, 'You know what you do to a man?'

'Ha!' She laughed, coquettishly, re-tying her bodice, and spun away, her skirt and underskirts rustling as they twirled. 'I can guess.'

Slaughter watched her go. *What is she, some kinda teaser?* he wondered.

However, he walked back to the house, helped himself

to another port, listened to the singing and decided it might have been a come-on. So he stole back into the house and along a corridor to a door he had earlier seen her come from. He rapped on it and waited for a kiss.

It was unbolted from inside and opened a few inches to reveal the undeniably ugly mug of her chaperon, her black hair pulled severely back from her gaunt face.

'Oh . . . uh . . . yuh . . . I was wondering which is my room?'

'Surely you did not imagine you would be sleeping in the house?' she hissed. 'Scum like you sleep with the *vaqueros*.'

There was a titter of laughter from inside as she slammed the door in his face and bolted it.

'Waal.' He tipped his hat over his eyes and scratched the back of his head. 'Whadda ya know?'

FIVE

In the morning he was back at the corral with Don
Miguel, watching as Ricardo led out his white mare and
Henry enthusiastically performed. He heard the rattle of
wheels and looked round to see the coachman pulling in
the four-wheeled phaeton behind them. Raquel, her
duenna of the rat-trap face sitting beside her, was looking
as fresh as a daisy in a white summer dress and straw hat,
alertly watching the proceedings.

'He's very good, isn't he?' she said, with a smile,
before telling the coachman to drive on.

That's about all I'm gonna get from that li'l minx,
Slaughter thought. Sarcasm. Still, on second thoughts
maybe it was just as well he hadn't abused his host's hospitality, for this morning Don Miguel was indeed toting a
shotgun.

'Going hunting?' he asked. 'There's a damn great
grizzly down by the lake. Charged me and Henry yesterday. Gave us quite a fright.'

'Oh, him, he's a bad one,' Don Miguel said. 'Comes
down from the mountains after my calves.'

'Don't he worry you?'

'Grizzlies have to eat.' Don Miguel gestured with his hands. 'To tell you the truth these days I feel it is certain humans who need hunting out, not bears.'

'Yeah?'

'Your money, Slaughter,' Ricardo announced, as he joined them. 'I am well pleased.' He counted out fifty dollars in coins. 'It will be interesting to see the colour of the foal.'

'Ain't you got any dollar bills?'

'Ha!' Ricardo bared his crossed teeth in a grin. 'Are you trying to trick me?'

Slaughter returned the grin. 'It's easier to carry, thassall. Well, one day you'll have a fine horse you can sell for two hundred dollars. So you'll have made a good profit. I'll give Henry some oats and a little rest, then we'll be on our way.'

'So long *señor*,' Don Miguel said. 'Good hunting.' He swung around, the shotgun aimed, perhaps accidentally, at Slaughter's groin, his dark eyes hard. 'I understand you have taken a fancy to my daughter. I warn you, don't. She is not for you.'

Slaughter put the stallion to a fast lope following a winding white trail east across the green prairie. Eventually he spotted the coach and pair of dun horses in front of him. The driver was upon the box and the two females down behind him.

'Howdy,' he called, touching his hatbrim to them as he rode alongside. 'Where you off to?'

'None of your business,' the chaperon snapped.

49

'Off on a shopping spree?' Slaughter asked, ignoring her. 'Going into Visalia to buy another new dress?'

Raquel smiled merrily across. 'No. As a matter of fact we are turning off along here. I am going to visit the Henderson ranch.'

'Henderson? I thought him and your father were daggers drawn.'

'They are. That's why I'm going, bearing an olive branch. I want to try to persuade Mr Henderson to come to a peaceful agreement with us.'

'Oh, yeah? How ya goin' to do that? Your old man seems convinced Henderson's a lowdown snake who's trying to steal his land and has been rustling his cows.'

'I'm not sure that's true. We are holding our rodeo – or round-up you Americans call it – when adjoining landowners get together to sort out whose beeves are whose. There's bound to be trouble. It could spark off range war. I want to try to make Mr Henderson see our point of view.'

'So that's why you're all duded up"

'A woman's wiles, you mean?' Raquel grabbed at her straw hat against a sudden gust of wind. 'I can only try.'

Slaughter jogged along beside her, his stallion holding his head and tail high as if proud of his morning's work. They were coming up to a gateway with, above it, the spider-shaped brand of the Tarantula ranch, Henderson's spread, the trail leading from it towards his homestead.

'Tarantula, huh? Sounds like it might suit him.'

'Dear, dear,' Raquel chided him with a smile. 'You're not jealous, are you, Mr Detective?'

'Maybe I should come in with you? You might need protection.'

'I don't need protection *by* you,' Raquel called. 'I need protection *from* you.'

'If you mean last night, I guess I was a bit over-enthusiastic. I musta misread the message.'

'Don't worry about it. Your half-hearted apology is accepted. Visalia is in that direction, Señor Slaughter.'

'Yeah, right, so long.' He watched them drive through the gate and head up the trail. 'You know, Henry, that gal's starting to bother me. What's she up to?'

Cattle had long reigned supreme in this part of California south of the San Joaquin valley. But the recent construction of the railroad had brought homesteaders to claim their eighty acres of free government land, or to buy 150 acres from the railroad company at two-and-a-half dollars an acre. In the equable climate the soil proved fertile and they raised fields of fourteen-feet high corn, or experimented with beans, hops, grapes, wheat, castor-oil presses, honey bees, silk worms, or even opium poppies, popular among the Chinese population. The railroad meant they could send their produce to the northern markets. So Visalia had grown from a dusty frontier town into a busy market and railroad centre.

To the east of the railroad were the slopes of the Sierra Nevada where a forest of the great sequoia extended in a stretch of 150 miles long by ten miles wide from Visalia all the way to Bakersfield. The loggers had moved in and they had begun dragging the great felled redwoods by teams of oxen down to the sawmills and railroad. Only the biggest of these magnificent sequoias – some 300 feet high by forty-three feet in diameter – were spared simply because the loggers did not, as yet, have the tools to tackle them.

Thus, the Mexican landowners with their feudal power, their airs and graces, who had once been lords of all they surveyed were fast becoming an anachronism in California, unwilling or unable to adapt to the modern, thrusting times.

The Welcome Stranger was the name of Visalia's main saloon. It was a big old barn of a place. There was an ornately carved billiards table at one end from which came the clicketing of balls as men gathered around. Others stood along the mahogany bar: farmers, railroadmen and traders discussing their day. In a corner a lady harpist was pinging out angelic harmonies with her fingers. On another some loudmouth rowdy was demolishing fast a bottle of whiskey and regaling whoever cared to listen with what he considered to be his fascinating life story.

'Let's face it,' he yelled, 'a cowboy's part-time occupation is rustling. How's he expected to exist on the thirty-a-month pittance the barons of beef pay him?'

He was a squat, muscular man in a check shirt, jeans, and spurred boots, his considerable girth cinched tight by a double-rigged gunbelt that pegged him as a hardcase.

'So, you admit you're a rustler?' one of his gawping listeners queried.

'Sure, let's say I did a bit. That was up in Oregon. Most cowhands up there have a weakness for other folks' cattle. I'd just gathered a nice li'l bunch in a canyon and had my runnin' iron in the fire when their owner jumped me. He took me into town as a warning to any others who might have the same idea, put me on trial, and, after passing round the whiskey the judge and jurors agreed I was guilty and should be hanged that day.'

'Quite right, too.' The town lawyer, Hilarius Bogbinder, a dapper, effete man, was standing a short distance away. 'What else did you expect?'

'Huh, well, I didn't agree. I busted outa that jail. But I wasn't leaving empty-handed. I rode back to that canyon to collect my cattle. Who should I bump into?'

'The rancher?'

'You guessed it, brother. He had the nerve to pull his gun on me again. I was forced to shoot him outa the saddle. So that's when I headed down to Californi-yey.'

'With the cattle?'

'Sure, but I sold 'em in Klamath Falls, Oregon, 'fore I crossed the border.'

The braggart, rosy-faced and sweating, paused to beam at his audience and took another swig from the neck of the bottle. He took off his high-crowned Stetson to reveal a shiny, white bald head, and mopped his brow with a bandanna.

'So you're wanted for homicide and rustling in Oregon?' Bogbinder, in his frock-coat, striped pants, shiny shoes and a diamond stick-pin in his cravat, stroked back his oily quiff. 'What's the price tag?'

'The reward? A measly four hundred dollars. I thought I might rate more than that.'

Some fellow nudged him and obviously told him that Bogbinder was a lawyer, for he grinned and asked, 'What about giving me your professional advice, pal? Should I jog on down to Mexico or am I safe here?'

'I generally charge for professional advice, but I really can't help you, my friend. You could apply to the governor for a pardon. What's your handle, by the way?'

'Hans Groper.' As some of the men laughed, he protested, 'No, it is. My daddy was a Dutchman.'

Mr Bogbinder stroked his pencil moustache with a manicured nail and gave a conceited smile. 'A dubious sobriquet.'

'Huh?' Hans demanded. 'What's he say?'

'My best advice to you is change your name and stay clear of Oregon.'

'Change my name,' Groper protested. 'I like my name.'

'Too bad.' Bogbinder shrugged, sipped the remains of his sweet port, then strolled over to the killer, putting an arm around his shoulder and directing him to a nearby table. 'A private word in your ear. If you're looking for work, Mr Henderson at the Tarantula ranch might be ready to take on a man who can tote a gun.'

'The Tarantula. Thanks, mister. Maybe I'll ride out there.'

As Slaughter rode in he noticed a stoutly built man in a tall Stetson on a sturdy grey heading in the direction from which he had come. 'Howdy,' he called, as the man waved to him.

He crossed the railroad line and swerved around

54

cattle corrals and lumber yards into an assemblage of stores, restaurant, church, and various buildings until he reached a livery. FEED AND STALL $1, a sign said, so he booked Henry in and bedded him down, slinging his saddle over a rail. He decided to leave his carbine in its boot while he took a stroll around.

When he reached the Welcome Stranger he hitched his Schofield back on one hip and pushed through the batwing doors, pausing to glance through slitted eyes at the throng, who appeared harmless enough. He found a space at the bar, put a toe on the brass footrail and waited for the 'keep to serve him. He seemed to be taking his time. He was a tall, stringy-haired individual in a long apron who more or less ignored him.

'Hey, bud, gimme a whiskey.'

'Didn't you see the sign?' The 'keep polished glasses and nodded at one that read, 'No dogs, Indians or Chinese'.

'I ain't none of them three,' Slaughter growled, 'so damn well move your backside.'

'There's the same sign outside,' the barman whined. 'This is a high-class establishment and we don't want no riffraff and drifters.'

'I'll give you ten seconds.' Slaughter pointed a finger at him. ' 'Fore I take this dump apart.'

'Hey, just what's going on?' Another tall man, his high-heeled boots and tall hat making him appear even taller, strode towards him. 'Who are you threatening?'

'Who the hell are you?'

Trick Loomis was neatly attired in a grey three-piece suit. He pulled back his jacket to reveal a tin star. 'I'm the sheriff of this town.'

'Yeah, well I advise you to keep out of this. It's between me and him. As a law-abiding citizen I am demanding my equal rights. And I'm starting counting.'

But before he could get to five a six-gun was jabbed into his spine.

'Thanks, Bob,' Loomis drawled to his deputy. He reached over to relieve Slaughter of his Schofield and placed it on the bartop. Then he frisked him, finding the private eye badge in his pocket. 'Aha, you must be the fella I've heard about.'

'News travels fast around here, huh? Who told you, one of Don Miguel's boys?'

'Serve him,' the sheriff said, handing back the wallet. 'But I should warn you, Southern Reb bounty hunters ain't welcome in this vicinity. Maybe you would like to pay me in advance for your pine coffin?'

'Very funny. Maybe you should change the name of this joint to the Unwelcome Stranger?' Slaughter swallowed half of the tumbler of whiskey, spat at a spittoon, narrowly missing the sheriff's boots, and gritted out, 'Maybe I should remind you, Sheriff, that this badge gives me federal backing and it's your duty to assist me in my enquiries. This is a serious crime we're talking about, gone unsolved on your patch.'

'Sure,' the sheriff sneered. 'And serious cash bounty for you, too, I'd wager. I'll repeat again, we don't cooperate with half-Injun drifter scum.'

Bogbinder gave an effeminate laugh. He had come to stand along one side. 'That's going a bit far, Trick. This fellow might have a case under the Bill of Rights.'

'I don't care what case he might have, Mister Lawyer.

56

I'm telling him he'll get no cooperation from me and I am strongly advising him to get out of this town pronto and go back to where he came from. If not, all I can say is, he's signing his own death certificate.'

'Lawyer? You must be this Mr Boghouse I've been hearing about.'

'Bogbinder. Really? And who's been telling tales about me? That old fool who still thinks he owns all the prairie? Don Miguel?'

'And you're the young fool, I presume, who thinks you can cheat him out of all he owns. You're stirring up a keg of trouble in this town, both of you. Purty soon it's gonna explode.'

'Oh, yes?' Bogbinder remarked, dismissively. 'So who's going to set the match?'

'Get lost and keep outa trouble,' Loomis growled. 'And don't say you ain't been warned.'

Slaughter reached for his revolver and slid it back in its holster. He had just noticed Aaron Snipe sitting at a table not far off in his new striped suit. The bowler hat was too big for his little head but was held up by his stick-out ears. There was a chubby lady by his side who kept emitting little giggles of glee. Maybe she'd had too much of Aaron's cough mixture.

He took his half-full glass. 'See you around, gents,' he called, as he ambled off. He gave Snipe a flicker of a wink as he sat at an adjoining table, stuck out his boots and lit one of Don Miguel's cigars.

'Ah,' he said to no one in particular as he blew a smoke ring, 'What a charming establishment. It's like kicking over a rock and finding a load of slimy, crawling reptiles underneath.'

The sheriff, his deputy and the lawyer glanced at him angrily, but decided to ignore him.

Snipe was stroking the pasty, rouge-tinged cheek of his middle-aged lady-friend, her big eyes goggling at him beneath her flower-topped hat. He snaked an arm around her blouse-clad back, his fingers groping for her bosom, but it wasn't there.

'Lower,' she stage-whispered. He finally found it down around the area of her navel, and bobbed a bloused breast in his hand with a smirk. She giggled again.

'That woman should be ashamed of herself,' the sheriff said. 'Her husband's hardly cold in his grave.'

Snipe grinned and got up to go the rounds with his carpetbag of bottles. Most men waved him away, but he made a few sales, returning in a circle past those at the bar until he reached Slaughter.

'Something to soothe that smoker's cough, sir?'

'Who's the old biddy?'

'Elspeth. Knocked on her cottage door selling my wares yesterday afternoon. I think ahm in lurve agin.' The widow gave another shrill giggle when he turned to her and brandished a clenched fist. 'We'll be going back to make her bedsprings squeal purty soon.'

'If it does that to her I'd better give it a try.'

Snipe lowered his voice. 'Seems like Henderson's recruiting hardmen. Bogsniffer's jest sent one out to join 'em. Looks like war.'

Slaughter dug in his pocket for a dollar as Aaron presented him with a little blue bottle. 'Anything else?' he asked.

'Thassall, thank you, sir.'

Slaughter tipped a few drops in his whiskey, somewhat against his better judgement, and when he stood up felt decidedly whoozy. 'Guess I better hit the hay with Henry,' he muttered.

He went out through the batwing doors and stood on the corner sidewalk, trying to remember the way to the livery. 'Oh, yeah, must be up there.' He headed across the dirt road, his footsteps oddly unsteady. Just as well they were for a carbine shot cracked out from up above just as he weaved to one side and the lead spurted mud from where he had intended to step.

Instinct made Slaughter leap for the safety of the far side of a horse trough, but he missed. He hauled out his Schofield in mid-air as another bullet shaved his heels, and he landed with a big splash in the trough. He went under as bullets peppered about him, waggling his revolver high to keep it dry and firing off a couple of shots wildly in the hoped-for direction of his would-be assassin.

He came up spitting out a mouthful of muddy muck and saw a black-smoke cloud drifting from one side of the Welcome Stranger's false front. His first shot went through the wood, his second splintered it some more. Suddenly a Mexican stepped out from behind it, a *vaquero* in a sombrero, his carbine, tight to his shoulder, spitting fire and lead.

Slaughter held his right arm outstretched, thumbing the hammer not twice, not thrice, but four times before his assailant took two steps forward and tumbled from the saloon roof to land on his back in the mud. The lieutenant put his last slug through his temple to make sure.

He climbed from the trough and staggered over,the smoking Schofield dangling from his fist. He looked down at the corpse's blood-splattered features before making the sign of the cross over him. 'Mino!'

The sheriff, Trick Loomis, had his revolver raised as he led men out from the saloon. A shopkeeper ran across shouting, 'This fella got bushwhacked. I saw it all. He's lucky to be alive.'

'I guess Mino'd got a grudge against me. Must admit I give him a clout or two yesterday for being naughty.' Slaughter's face split into a grin and he giggled just like Snipe's lady. 'Funny, innit? Didn't think he'd take it so personal.'

'Don't say I didn't warn you,' the sheriff growled.

'Yeah, but I didn't know hostilities would start so soon. Hang on, this is *my* Spencer.' He picked up the carbine from the ground and brandished it. 'Friggin' cheek. He musta nicked it from my saddle boot. I coulda been slain by my own gun.'

Bogbinder had joined them at the scene and put in, 'This man might have informed us about you earlier today, but don't get the idea this was anything to do with us. We didn't set him on you.'

'Ha! I'm all wet!' Slaughter started braying like a mule with raucous laughter. 'Haaaagh!' He slapped the lawyer on his back, nearly knocking him off his feet. 'I ain't saying you did, Hilarius. It's hilarious, ain't it, you ol' bogcleaner.'

The lawyer quickly moved out of the way as Slaughter slung the carbine over his shoulder and staggered away towards the livery, giving them a farewell wave of his pistol.

'What's the matter with *him?*'

'Funny,' Loomis muttered. 'Looks like he's been hitting the happy juice. We gotta get rid of that guy. He's getting on my nerves.'

SIX

The 'medicine' might not have cured his cough, but it certainly made him sleep. He woke up in the hay of the stallion's stall in the early morning and became aware that four pairs of unangelic eyes were looking down at him.

'Wake up, you Tucson pig,' Deputy Bob Olliphant snarled, thudding his boot into the former sheriff's side as his two fellow deputies started doing likewise.

'We're arresting you for murder,' Sheriff Loomis shouted, prodding him hard with the dangerous end of the Spencer carbine. 'Get on your feet.'

'I'm trying to,' Slaughter gasped, grabbing the heel of Olliphant's boot. He jerked his foot forward and hit his knee to lever him backwards. He caught hold of the Spencer barrel and pulled it from Loomis's hands, swinging it to slam across the side of one of his attackers, and back to crack against the other's jaw.

Now he was able to spring to his feet. He lunged at Olliphant with the carbine, knocking him sprawling. But the deputy who had been hit in the side was tougher than he looked. He had grabbed a length of discarded plough chain and swung it to wind around Slaughter's windpipe, pulling it to half-choke him. Sheriff Loomis had stepped in, too, seizing the carbine's butt. He tore it from Slaughter's grip.

With a howl of grief Slaughter swung haymakers right, left and centre as more kicks and blows thudded into his face and his gut. The four men were too much for him, gripping his arms and dragging him away as the stallion shrieked his anger and kicked out at them, too.

The carbine barrel was pressed hard into Slaughter's throat as his arms were twisted back and Sheriff Loomis levered the Spencer to slide a round into the chamber. He leered at Slaughter. 'I could shoot you for resisting arrest.'

'Go on, Trick,' Olliphant urged. 'Kill him.'

'I wish I could, but it wouldn't look good.'

'Go on,' one of the others said. 'Nobody never got hanged fer killin' an Indian. You'd be doing the community a favour.'

'Bloodthirsty li'l bastard, ain't he?' Slaughter tried to grin defiantly as blood trickled from his lip. 'How many times I got to tell ya I ain't an Indian?'

'It's him who'll hang, but this time legally,' Loomis declared. 'Cuff him and chain him, boys.'

'You c—!' Slaughter lunged his moccasined foot and caught the sheriff hard in his 'inflatables', making him double up in agony. 'That's too good a word for you. It's a useful part of the female anatomy.'

His defiance only earned him an even more severe pummelling and booting, if that were possible, and

Sheriff Loomis lurched after them, a hand between his legs, as they dragged Slaughter away to the jailhouse.

The Visalia town judge, Dr Ian Dixon, was a fidgety little man, seated on a dais in the courthouse as James Slaughter was brought before him two days later for an inquest into the death of Mino Florio.

'Why is this witness in chains?' he asked, ignoring the obvious signs of the beating Slaughter had endured.

'Because, your honour, I wish to press a charge of first degree homicide against him.' Sheriff Loomis didn't look so tall without his Stetson but, with his big moustache, and in his clerical grey suit he still struck an imposing stance. 'The victim, of course, being Señor Florio.'

'I'm sorry, Trick, you can't just ride roughshod over the law,' Dr Dixon muttered, glancing nervously from Loomis to the jury panel and noting the presence of the editor of the *Visalia Plainspeaker* with his pencil and notebook at the ready. 'We must hear the verdict of the inquest jury before we decide upon that.'

'Quite right,' Slaughter put in. 'You lot ain't gonna railroad me.'

'Silence,' Deputy Olliphant snarled. 'Speak when you're spoken to, thassall.'

'Right, as you admit you killed this man I'll take your evidence first.'

'He took a pot at me from the rooftop as I came outa the saloon,' Slaughter drawled. 'So I defended myself.'

Dixon sighed and requested more detail. Then he called the shopkeeper to the box, and a couple of other

64

bystanders at the time, who backed Slaughter's words.

There was a small crowd of onlookers in the court-house, who, as the jury considered their verdict, noisily joined in the discussion.

'Seems like a cut an' dried case of self-defence, your honour,' the foreman drawled. 'Cain't say no more.'

'I disagree.' The sheriff tried to be heard above derisive laughter. 'I contend the prisoner deliberately provoked and pursued Señor Florio with malice afore-thought, intending to kill him.'

'Rubbish!' Aaron Snipe hooted. 'He was three sheets to the wind when he left the saloon. Not that I know the man. I just sold him a bottle of my excellent cough med-icine. Heard him say he was gonna go and sleep it off.'

There was more laughter as Dr Dixon banged his gavel, trying to keep order and Sheriff Loomis bellowed, 'I demand James Slaughter be tried for first degree murder. We oughta hang him high. The man's a trou-blemaker. Nobody will be safe in their beds if he's allowed to go free.'

Suddenly Ricardo de Estudillo Puyol rose from the crowd, his silver-embroidered sombrero in his hands. 'May I be allowed to speak? Mino Florio left my father's *rancho* yesterday after boasting to our men that he was going to kill Señor Slaughter. I can swear to that.'

There was a surprised silence as Dixon asked, 'Was there bad blood between the two men?'

'They had a minor scrap or disagreement but Señor Slaughter never showed any indication that he intended to pursue it further. It was over as far as he was con-cerned. Whereas Mino, he was a hothead. He had

65

already tried to knife Slaughter.'

'Why did Florio do that?'

'He didn't like gringos.'

This caused more uneasy laughter and Dixon made a downturned grimace at the sheriff. 'There are certain statutes in California that I am forced to observe, even here in Visalia that prevent me granting your application, Sheriff. My verdict is self-defence. The prisoner will not stand trial for murder.'

'Thanks judge,' Slaughter drawled. 'Can you tell me, are you a doctor of philosophy or of medicine?'

Dixon regarded him sharply. 'I was a doctor of medicine before my retirement. Why, what has that got to do with you?'

'So, when did you retire?'

'A year ago, if it is any business of yours. Release this man, Deputy Olliphant. He is free to go.'

'The court will rise,' the sheriff shouted, and scowled as he watched Dixon grab his papers and scuttle away.

The deputy reluctantly released Slaughter from his chains. Slaughter then eased his wrists and regarded the law officers through narrowed lids. 'Don't think you're getting away with this. Next time I'll be ready for you.'

'And us for you,' Olliphant replied.

'So, I'll be needing my weapons back.'

'I've never seen such a miscarriage of justice,' Sheriff Loomis bellowed, as he grabbed his hat. 'Give the man back his guns, Deputy. Let him go out and cause more mayhem. Listen, you people. Yes it's *us* who will be waiting for him. I intend to stand by my badge and the oath I swore to protect this community.'

'Ach, belt up, you windbag.' Slaughter turned to Ricardo and shook his hand. 'Hey there, *caballero*. I'm gonna buy you and me a beer.'

The Devil's Cauldron it read, painted in red above the bead-curtained doorway of the bar in the Latino quarter.

'Sounds like you can have some hot times here,' Slaughter said, as they stepped inside.

'No, the hottest thing is the food.' The youth gave his flashing cross-fanged grin. 'We Mexicans like exotic names.'

The three-foot thick adobe walls kept the place cool and in the shady interior there were comfortable armchairs, an assortment of tables and a solid bar behind which a tall young woman, her thick black hair drawn back tight against her skull and held by a crimson scarf, reigned.

'*Buenos dios*, Anna,' Ricardo called. 'Meet my *amigo*, James.'

'Howdy, 'Slaughter drawled. 'What's it to be, Ricky?'

'*Americano*, huh?' Anna was cleaning glasses and Slaughter noticed her carmine nails and the mockery glowing in her eyes. 'If you are with Ricardo you are welcome.'

She poured a tequila with lime juice for the youth and a beer from a barrel for Slaughter, popping in a chunk of ice from a bucket and giving it a stir. He watched the movement of her deep, maternal breasts in her off-the-shoulder blouse, nestled there like a couple of plump doves. A loose scarlet skirt was tied with a sash about her ample hips.

'Why's he giving me that look?' she asked. 'Hasn't he seen a woman before?'

'Not one like you.' Slaughter took a swig of the beer and continued giving her the once over. He gave a gasp of pleasure. 'This is great after being stuck in that damn cell for two days.'

'You have a jailbird for a friend, Ricardo? I am surprised at you. That look in his eye means he's hungry for food or the other thing. You had better tell him this is not that sort of place.'

'I'll settle for food,' Slaughter replied in her own language for there was an appetizing scent emanating from a back kitchen. 'For the time being.'

'Calm down, *señor*. How about a two-pound rainbow trout fresh from the lake?'

'Sounds just the ticket.'

'Goose in tabasco sauce for Ricardo. I know what he likes.'

'Not too hot,' the young man called as they found a table.

'Yeah, Mexican food comes in two flavours,' Slaughter recalled. 'Hot, or hot as hell. And she's some hot *tamale* herself. Is she the bargirl or does she own the joint?'

'She's the owner, but I believe the sheriff takes his cut.'

'Yeah?'

'In this town Loomis and Bogbinder take a share of most things. That lawyer is so crooked when he dies they will have to screw his coffin to the ground.'

'How about the judge?'

'He is either in their pay or they have him running scared.'

68

'I'd like to question Dixon some more. Where's he hang out?'

'He has a big villa on the outskirts of town, lives there with his widowed daughter and grandchildren. You can't miss it, a two-storey place, red tiles on the roof, a bougainvillaea hanging over the wall.'

'So, you figure those three are the ones behind the robbery?'

'Most people are of that opinion, but they dare not say so.'

'Yeah?' Slaughter eyed the young Mexican. 'One thing seems certain; whoever did it is not in dire need of the cash. They must have plenty in the bank already and are biding their time.'

'That is true, unless they already have it in some secret account someplace like New York. You know what these crafty lawyers are like.'

'You don't seem to be short of a few pesos yourself. That silver enscrolled revolver of your's. Are those real rubies in the grip? It must be worth five hundred bucks. And that saddle with the gold horn – I'm surprised it ain't been stolen.'

'Ah, you are trying to trap me again. I have two of my men outside guarding my horse. I would not come into town alone. You must remember my father has become a very wealthy man since the Americans arrived in California. There is a lot of money in the cattle business.'

'He seems to be a very lackadaisical man, if you know what I mean. I think the French call it an air of *laissez-faire.*'

'*Sí*, of course he prefers the old easygoing Spanish

69

ways. Naturally he avoids banks in case the Americans cheat him. He has his cash stashed away in gold and silver coin. I doubt if he knows how much he has or exactly where it is.'

'Yes, but if he loses his land all that could all end. You must know, Ricardo, many rich Mexicans have been stripped of their assets by the courts.'

Ricardo nodded and tossed back another shot of tequila. 'I know that. It is a worry to my sister and me.'

'Is your mother still alive? I ain't seen any sign of her.'

'Yes, she is very much alive. She suffers from religious mania. She lives in the room in the tower. There is a miniature chapel in there: candles burning, statues of angels and shrines to the saints. She has her meals taken up to her. She is more or less a recluse.'

'So I expect your old man has to seek female fun and frolics in other quarters?'

Ricardo gave a scoffing laugh. 'I don't think so. He must be past all that.'

'He ain't that old.'

'Come on, James.' Ricardo gave him his cross-toothed grin. 'Why so many questions?'

'It's my job to ask questions.' Slaughter gave a shrug. 'Just one more. Do you know any fellow around here called Frank?'

'Frank? No. I can't say I do. I went with my sister to the public school here and I know many of the townspeople casually. Of course, there is the wagon-maker, he's Frank. And one of the farmers. But they are above suspicion. I am sorry I cannot be of more help.'

'Thass OK, Ricky. Maybe I'll try one of them tequila

70

and limes myself. You've been a great help.'

'I want you to solve this case and get out of this town while you can. I would hate to see you killed, *amigo*.'

'Yeah, me, too. So that's why you both speak good English. You picked it up at school?'

'Of course. But there is bad blood between the Anglos and us former Mexicans. We are supposed to be American citizens now but we are treated as a second-rate caste. Only the Chinese and the Indians are treated worse than us but they can hardly defend themselves. My *vaqueros* do not suffer insults lightly.'

'I know what it's like,' Slaughter said. 'Don't tell me.'

They lapsed into silence and enjoyed their drinks until Anna brought the food. Slaughter put an arm around her as she served them and patted her sturdy thigh, fancying he felt something hard beneath the skirt. She shoved him off with one hip and skipped away, leaving him to it.

'Is she packing somethang?'

'What do you mean? Ah, yes, she keeps a stiletto strapped to her thigh in case of trouble.'

'I'll remember that.'

'A good looking woman, huh?'

'She sure ain't ugly,' the lieutenant muttered between mouthfuls. 'You figure I could get to know her?'

'I see no reason why not. She is not my property.'

'I mean has she any other beau? Don't wanna step on anybody's toes.'

'I do believe,' Ricardo replied in a lowered tone, 'she and Sheriff Loomis had something going at one time. But she is a very independent lady.'

71

'In that case maybe I'll call back tonight. By the way, are you aware that the rancher, Henderson, is recruiting gunslingers?'

'I am very much aware of that.'

They sat in silence until they were replete, when Ricardo leaned back, regarded Slaughter and said, 'We, too, could do with some fast guns. Would you be interested in working for my father, James? He would pay you well.'

'Aw, no. I'm gettin' old, hittin' thirty,' Slaughter drawled. 'I'm retired from that kinda thang. I'm just here to do the job I was sent to do, or try to. Thassall. I'm sorry, pal. You'll have to fight your own battles.'

Slaughter pulled in his stallion outside the iron gate of the red-tiled mansion and clanged on a bellpull. When a black servant appeared he said, 'I wanna have a few words with the judge.'

The man returned to say, 'The judge ain't receiving visitors especially not men of your ilk. Those were his words.'

'Is that so?' Slaughter trotted Henry around to the side, jumped up on the saddle, nimbly climbed over the wall and leapt lightly down into a shrubbery. There were two children, about ten or eleven years old playing in the nearby yard with a big hound dog.

Suddenly the dog spotted the intruder and charged across like a cannonball to leap at him, snarling and salivating, biting his fangs into his left arm, nearly knocking him over.

Slaughter had come prepared for such an eventuality;

a bandanna wrapped around his wrist under his leather coat and over his riding glove. 'Geddown, you brute,' he snarled back, wrestling with the animal. He found a chunk of meat soaked in whiskey in his right pocket and waggled it under the hound's nose. 'Here y'are. Catch.'

When the dog leaped to catch it Slaughter tossed him another chunk to keep him busy and, raising a finger to his mouth to the watching boys, slipped through an open window into the house.

He crossed a shady, stone-floored lobby towards what looked like a study. Through the partly open door he could see a bookcase against a wall.

'Excuse me barging in unannounced, Judge,' he drawled as he stepped inside, 'but I wanna ask you a couple of questions.'

Dixon leapt from his armchair like a scalded cat. 'What? Get out of here. I'll have you arrested for unlaw-ful—'

'Yeah, sure, simmer down.' He shoved Dr Dixon back into his chair and showed him his badge. 'I'm working for the Pinkerton agency as you no doubt know. I got a coupla questions and I'd like straight answers.'

'How dare you?' The doctor tried to get to his feet but Slaughter tipped him back into the chair.

'Just listen, will ya? Did you in the past twelve months remove a bullet from the shoulder of a man who was brought here?'

'What are you saying? You trying to implicate me in that train robbery?'

'OK, that's what we're talking about here. More pre-cisely, six months ago, did you give medical treatment to one of those fugitives?'

'I have no intention of answering your questions, you villain. I intend to see you thrown back in jail where you belong.'

'C'm on, Judge. Don't prevaricate. Just give me a straight answer, yes or no.'

'*No*,' Dr Dixon shouted. 'Is that good enough for you? Now get out of my house.'

'No?' Slaughter studied him. 'To tell the truth I don't believe you.'

'*You* don't believe *me*? Might I remind you I am a respected doctor and judge. What are you? Some damned prairie rat bounty hunter? What do you think gives you the right to question me?'

Slaughter waggled the Pinkerton badge. 'This gives me the right. This has got federal backing. Don't try to brand me as a thug. In my opinion you're in with the thugs who run this town, who, also, in my opinion I suspect of being behind the robbery. If you are it makes you no better than a thug yourself.'

'Nonsense. You're a madman. Clear off back to Tucson where you belong. I wouldn't advise—'

'I ain't interested in what you'd advise, Doc.'

Outside the study he found a woman standing in the lobby. 'What's going on?' she demanded.

Dixon had followed him. 'The gentleman's just leaving, Daughter.'

Slaughter eyed her. She was in her late thirties, flaxen of hair, respectably attired in a grey skirt and a blouse pinned by a cameo at the throat. 'I'll show him out,' she said. 'Through the door this time.'

She was obviously the mother of the two boys. 'What have you done to Bruno?' she demanded.

The hound wobbled wonkily towards them, collapsed on his side and yawned. 'Aw, he'll be OK. He's had a bit too much. He'll sleep it off. So long to y'all.'

The black servant opened the front gate and Slaughter gave a whistle for Henry. The woman followed him out, glancing behind at the house, her face and eyes agitated.

'I overheard what went on in the study,' she said. 'I'm very worried about Dad. He's in trouble. I know that. But he won't admit it because he's frightened of what they might do to me and the children. I have heard them threaten him.'

'Who? The sheriff? The lawyer?'

'Both of them. They are evil men. Dad is terrified of them.'

'So, did your father treat one of those robbers?'

'I don't know. I wasn't here. You had better go.' She started backing away. 'I can't tell you any more.'

'You mean you won't?' The stallion had trotted back to him and he swung into the saddle, swirling him around. 'OK. Don't worry. I can do without your father's testimony. I got enough to work on.' He rode away, giving a backward wave of his hand.

SEVEN

Ricardo de Estudillo Puyol was riding his spirited white Arab, the sun flashing on its gold and silver trappings, his two *vaquero* bodyguards alongside, heading out of town.

'Hey, *hombre*,' he shouted, when he and the men met Slaughter leaving the doctor's residence. 'What did you find out?'

'Not a lot.' Slaughter had his work cut out holding Henry back when the stallion spotted the mare. 'Maybe I oughta get one of them spiked erection deterrents you Mexicans use to strap around the hoss's private parts.'

'Ach, we are no longer so cruel.' Ricardo smiled. 'Why do you not join us and come to the rodeo tomorrow? Both you and Henry can have some fun.'

'That's an offer we cain't refuse.' As the stallion reared on his hind legs, kicking and whinnying, Slaughter hauled him around. 'Calm down, boy. You hear that? You'll be gettin' ya oats later.'

As they all left the town at a spirited lope, he added, 'That's more than I will. I was planning on calling in on the comely Anna tonight.'

'She will still be there tomorrow,' Ricardo said with a laugh. 'Let's give them a gallop. See who's the best.'

He gave a wild whoop as he went haring away on his mare and Henry didn't need any say-so to chase after her. It was a pounding, exhilarating gallop for several miles along the winding dust trail, and a near thing in the end, Slaughter just managing to send Henry spurting past on a wide bend to take the lead.

The two *vaqueros* galloped their mustangs up to join them as they slowed their pace and Ricardo introduced them.

'This,' he cried, waving to a weather-worn older man in a big sombrero, a rifle slung across his back, 'is my father's *mayordomo* – ramrodder to you – Raoul.'

The man nodded. A vivid white scar creased his dark cheek and his thin black moustachios drooped down past his chin. He didn't seem the friendly type.

'And that ugly dog is Adolpho. I should warn you, he is an expert with rope and knife.'

'I can believe it,' Slaughter said, eyeing a machete hanging from the similarly sullen *vaquero's* belt. 'They seem like a bundle of fun.'

Soon they reached the northern shore of the great lake with the King River which divided the Mexicans' estate from Henderson's, estuarying into it. They ploughed their horses through the river and on the other side Ricardo jumped down, hauled off his saddle and allowed the sweating mare to have a thorough bathe.

Slaughter and the others followed suit, then sat around smoking and watching otters splashing in the lake. 'We hunt them for their fur,' Ricardo remarked.

ɔok to the air as they set off again on the next
ride to the ranch house, soaring away over
as the four riders loped along beside the
ke. Ricardo pointed to some cattle and calves
on some low-lying hills and shouted, 'They will have to be
brought in. They are not Henderson's.'

The Laguna rancho had lost its calm air and was a hive
of activity for a General Beale, who owned the Tejun
ranch, a big spread south of Don Miguel's land, on the
western side of the lake, had arrived with his *vaqueros* to
take part in the springtime rodeo. As each man needed
six horses to carry out his work a lot of dust was being
kicked up. The Indian servants and cooks were more
than busy feeding them all. An ox was being roasted on
a spit and the juicy slices handed around on platters.

With his old-fashioned courtesy Don Miguel welcomed Slaughter to join him on his patio, where he
poured glasses of white wine which he said was made by
a German in his vineyard at Visalia.

'Why don't you make your own?' the general boomed
out at him.

The Don gave his laconic shrug. 'Why bother when I
can buy this in town?'

General Beale, a well-fed, hearty individual appeared
to be part-Spanish, part-Anglo by birth and was attired
and spoke in an odd mixture of both languages. 'How is
your good lady?' he asked.

'Ach!' Don Miguel made a down-turned grimace.
'Katerina was wed to Jesus many years ago. The only
other male visitor she welcomes is the priest.'

'That must be very hard for you.'

'I am *muy contento*. Or would be if it were not for that lawyer snapping at my heels. He is after my land.'

'It might be a good idea to get yourself an independent lawyer, say from Bakersfield,' Slaughter put in. 'I've heard there's one or two of your own race who would defend you.'

'Pah! Lawyers cost money. Very much money.'

The general boomed with laughter. 'You can afford it. Didn't you tell me you sold eighteen hundred young colts earlier this year?'

'*Sí*, but my son and daughter spent most of that gold for me.' He stared glumly at his glass. 'I wish I could have had several sons. My wife, however, abandoned such activities when she married the Lord many years ago. Now it is too late for me.'

'Your friend here speaks the truth,' the general said. 'You must get a lawyer to defend yourself.'

For reply Don Miguel pulled a revolver from his sash and fired it into the air, making several of his ranch hands jump around to see what was going on. He scowled at them. 'The only law I believe in is the law of the gun.'

Suddenly a window in the tower above them opened and a pointy-nosed woman with wild white hair poked out her head.

'What's going on?' she screamed. 'Can I have no quiet for my prayers?'

'Quick!' Don Miguel urged his Indian helper to pull back his chair and he did so with surprising alacrity. 'Get out of the way!'

'Oh, it's you,' his hag of a wife screamed, brandishing

a chamberpot. 'I've warned you about this.'

Slaughter quickly backed away to follow the *ranchero* into safety. But the general was not fast enough and as he scrambled after them was splattered with the contents of the pot.

'Eugh!' he said, wiping the odiferous excrement from his hair. 'This is the last time I'm coming here.'

The *vaqueros* were out before first dawn light and began to rake through the expansive pastures and hills on the borders of Don Miguel's lands to bring in the half-wild longhorns, joined now by cowboys from his northern neighbour, Don Alphonso Pico, a relative of the last Spanish governor of the state, who owned 100,000 acres.

Slaughter spent a leisurely day and, late in the afternoon, was grooming Henry in his corral. He decided to show a few Indians and pensioners who were watching a stunt or two. He had a simple hackamore on the stallion and, standing in the centre, sent him with a flick of his rope cantering around in a circle. He took a dash to leap on to his bare back landing on his feet, balancing at a stand, before dropping astride, slapping the horse's neck to make him prance faster. He jumped to his feet again before dropping down back to front. He glimpsed some Indian kids laughing so grinned, got hold of the horse's tail, and waved at them as he played the fool.

He pretended to fall off, but did a back flip and landed on his feet, took another run at the horse, missed his footing and bounced back, but he persevered and landed on his back the next time round. Slowing the horse to a stroll, he rewarded him with a handful of sugar.

'Very impressive,' a voice called in Spanish and. Slaughter looked across the rail to meet the teasing blue eyes of Raquel. Today she was garbed in a stiff-brimmed hat and riding habit, her long skirt covering her legs to the ankles as she sat, stately of posture, sidesaddle.

'So you can ride.' He slipped from Henry's high back. 'Thought you always travelled by coach.'

'It's the only way to escape from my duenna.' She smiled, sitting her well-schooled gelding, and laughed as the stallion came up behind the American, dipped his nose between his legs, and tossed him up into the air.

The children giggled as Slaughter went forward with exaggerated bowlegs and Henry tossed him high a couple of times more.

'You've taught him well.'

'Just having a bit of fun. Showin' off my Comanche blood.' He slung an arm around the eighteen-hands of Henry's powerful neck. 'Only possible due to his love of sugar lumps.'

'*Andale*!' she cried, riding back towards the house. 'We are going out to the rodeo ground.'

When he had saddled up, Slaughter found Don Miguel being helped into the saddle of a sprightly mustang, his feeble, half-paralysed legs roped to the stirrups, and with the other rancheros and his daughter, son and entourage around, went off at a fast lick out to the plain. By then thousands of cattle had been brought in to this control point, the calves plaintively following the cows, the bulls forced to comply by the sharp lances of the *vaqueros*.

Most of the hard work of cutting out, roping and

branding had already been done. Now was the time, with the rancheros watching, for the *vaqueros* to indulge in competitive display of their riding skills.

The onlookers applauded as a cowboy chased a bull out of the field, dashed after it at full speed and leant from the saddle to catch the tail of the fleeing beast. This he wound quickly about his hand, then tucked it between his leg and the saddle to hold it. Instantly the horse knew to increase its speed, passing the bull to fling it over its head, toppling to the ground. The rider then leapt from the saddle and held it ready for branding.

Other riders from the different outfits weaved their spirited mounts in among the cattle to single out a beast by its mark, then headed it adroitly out of the mass. Another horseman was ready to drive it to the knot of beeves where it belonged, the calf frantically running after its mother.

Most there enjoyed the good-humoured sport between the *vaqueros*. The one outfit that didn't join the competition was the Tarantula. Its cowboys didn't go in for grabbing tails. They used the more rough and ready American bulldogging method, leaping from the saddle to wrestle a cow or calf to the ground. They sat their horses and watched sullenly, as if the Mexicans' wild, whooping antics were beneath them.

Slaughter noticed that a man on a black horse had arrived. He was attired in funereal black, with a low-crowned black hat.

'Who's that character?' he asked. 'A preacher?'

'No, that's Henderson,' Raquel replied. 'I will invite

him to join our party.'

She sent her mount spurting across to the far side of the mob of cattle and appeared to converse with the rancher, who shook his head. 'The pious-looking bastard's declined the invitation,' Slaughter muttered.

Two other unwelcome characters had arrived: Bob Olliphant and another Visalia deputy. Olliphant also had that arrogant attitude of white superiority as he led his sidekick on horseback around the gathering and paused in front of Slaughter. 'What you doing here?' he asked.

'I could ask the same question of you.'

'We're making sure there ain't no trouble,' Olliphant snarled, and rode on.

Raquel had just rejoined the rancheros' party when there was a sudden outburst of raised voices and curses. Two men were pushing and shoving each other. One was a wiry, sharp-featured puncher, who seemed to be the Tarantula foreman; the other was one of Don Miguel's *vaqueros*.

'That's our brand, clear as day,' the Anglo stormed. 'You thievin' greaser, git your rope off it.'

'You son of a whore,' the Latino shouted back. 'You lie in your teeth.' He backed away, coiling his bullwhip and sent it cracking out to snap around the Tarantula man's throat. 'May your lies choke you.'

'Toss that whip away,' Hans Groper suddenly roared. 'Or it will be the last thing you do.'

He was standing about twenty paces away with both his twin .45s in his hands, aimed at the *vaquero*'s heart.

Immediately all the men about him, both Anglos and

83

Mexicans, went for their guns, their circle like a powder keg about to explode, bristling with antagonism on both sides. But the Tarantula gunmen were well-outnumbered. If Groper didn't back down there could well be a massacre.

The burly Dutchman stood over the roped steer in question and glared at his adversary. 'This is our cow and we're taking it,' he growled.

Don Miguel had charged over. 'Drop that whip,' he ordered the the *vaquero*. 'We are not going to argue about one cow. They can take it and go.'

Groper looked back to the figure in black watching from the shade of a huge oak. Henderson turned his steed, raised a gloved hand and headed back to his ranch.

'Come on, boys,' Groper sneered. 'We'll leave these dagoes to their stupid fun and games.'

'Yeah.' The ramrodder soothed his smarting neck. 'We'll gather up our cows and follow along.'

Slaughter watched them go, driving their reclaimed strays, followed by the two deputies. 'They weren't exactly the life and soul of the party, were they?' he remarked.

The scar-faced *mayordomo*, Raoul, spat in the dust. 'We should have taken our chance, killed them all.'

'My father too easily capitulated,' Ricardo commented. 'Where is his pride? The old man has become a weak fool. If we allow the gringos to trample over us they will be back again. If he goes on like this we will lose everything.'

*

84

However, a powder keg incident like that didn't dampen the *vaqueros*' spirits. That night after they had feasted, the guitars and castanets started strumming and clicketing as the women and girls of the house, dressed in their finery, swirled silken underskirts as they whirled, their partners strutting like feisty bantams, arms aloft, heels stamping, silver spurs jingling, amid whoops of appreciation.

Slaughter noted that Raquel was not among them. The night before she had attended the banquet for the visiting rancheros, in her satin dress and diamonds, the centre of attention. She had paid the lieutenant little heed, just occasionally flashing flirtatious eyes at him.

'Guess she's given me the bum's rush,' he said to himself as he left the laughter and carousing and went to check on his stallion in the corral.

He heard the sound of a horse and rider coming from Don Miguel's stable. To his surprise he saw in the moonlight Raquel, still in her riding apparel, wheel in a half circle and go galloping away across the dark prairie.

'Well, whaddda ya know? Where's she slippin' away to in such a fine hurry?' Slaughter scratched his jaw, then slung his saddle over the stallion's back. 'There's only one way to find out. Come on, boy, let's go.'

He, too, went streaking away, giving Henry a free rein, but not wanting to get too close to the dark distant figure illumined by the glow of a full melon moon which was climbing high. His quarry had circumnavigated the central plain where he could see the pinprick glow of cigarettes smoked by the men left to guard the restless cattle overnight. She swept down a slope and headed towards a line of low hills which, with the King River, demarcated

85

the two *estancias*. What was she heading that way for at this time of night?

As she reached the last clump of big oaks before the hills began Raquel suddenly swirled to a halt and jumped to the ground. Slaughter did likewise, keeping low. He could hardly believe his eyes when he saw a man, unmistakably attired in a black frock-coat, recognizable as Henderson even at that distance, step out from the trees' shadows.

'Well, I'll be a monkey's aunt,' the bounty hunter exclaimed, fumbling for his pocket telescope.

He trained it on them as they embraced, their faces meeting in a long-winded soul kiss until they broke apart and appeared to be deep in conversation. 'If only I could hear what they're saying.'

He guessed that that might be obvious. The answer to his question was the ages-old one: a passionate assignation. That became even more obvious when the duo set to kissing again and the rancher groped her thigh, pulling up her long riding-skirt.

Slaughter snapped shut the telescope. 'Ain't no point in playing the peeping Tom, is there?' Indeed, the couple, arms about each other's waists, were ducking under the boughs of the oak and had disappeared into darkness. 'No points for guessing what their next moves are gonna be.'

It was midnight when Raquel clipped in on her mustang at her father's stable. As she quickly unsaddled and settled her horse into a stall Slaughter rose from a bed of straw.

'Howdy,' he drawled. 'Had a nice moonlight ride? Or,

should I say, did Henderson enjoy his ride, if you get my meaning?'

'What?' She turned on him, startled, and slashed him across the face with her riding crop. 'How dare you, you foul-mouthed oaf!'

Slaughter put his hand to the stinging cut. 'You wanna play rough, huh?' He grabbed her by her blouse at the throat with one hand, twisting the quirt from her grasp with the other. He tossed it away and brought his hand back to give her a sharp slap across her cheek. 'Oh, yuh, I dare, don't worry. I wanna know what's going on. So, spill the beans, lady.'

Raquel gave a scream. Nobody had ever dared hit her before. But the Mexicans were too busy singing and dancing on into the night to hear, or pay any heed if they did. Now the brutal American was shaking her by her blouse front like a puppy. 'Come on, out with it.'

'All right.' Her coarse, corn-coloured hair had fallen down over face. 'Leave me alone. I'll tell you.'

He let her get her breath back and she stuttered out, 'I can't see what it's got to do with you. As you appear to know, Mr Henderson and I are lovers. He has promised to marry me. Does that satisfy you?'

'Yeah, but—'

'Ah, I see,' she cried, scornfully, tearing herself away from him. 'You are jealous. Yes, don't deny it. You thought you could have your filthy way with me. What possessed you to imagine I would want some crawling, spying snake of a useless, moneyless drifter to touch me? Look at yourself, man. You disgust me.'

'Yeah, well—'

'So,' she cried, tossing her hair back, haughtily, 'you may as well know I need a man of substance, with a future, who can look after me in the manner I—'

'And you're worried your old man is gonna lose his estates. So you're simply looking after your future, is that it?'

'Of course. Now, if you will step out of my way.' She waved him aside regally. 'I do not intend to mention your attack on me to my father. Think yourself lucky. If I did you would not find your death very pleasant, believe me.'

'Yeah, sure, piss off.'

Raquel hurried away but when she reached the door of the stable she turned and called out, 'You did not really imagine I would want a man like you?'

'A good question,' he shouted back.

But when she had gone he muttered to himself, 'There's something about this don't add up.' Then he grinned and opened his arms wide. 'Like, how can anybody resist me?'

EIGHT

When Slaughter shaved his stone-grey jaw with a cut-throat in the morning he peered into a small cracked mirror hanging on the wash-house wall. 'Maybe she's got a point,' he allowed, his face again splitting into a wide grin.

The girl's withering contempt of him had given him a restless night. Yes, perhaps he was a tad jealous of Henderson having his way with her. 'I seem to be the only one round here who ain't gittin' his oats,' he mused. Nonetheless, there had been more to his anger. Yes, there was more to Raquel than met the eye. For instance, her hair colour.

He rustled up a coffee in the house kitchen. The *vaqueros* had been out since first light, those from the adjoining *ranchos* collecting their cattle and heading home.

'Maybe it's time I went to see what this Henderson guy's got to say for himself,' he said to Henry as he jerked tight his saddle cinch and fastened the latigo strap.

They set off across the rolling parkland, passing the

clump of oaks where the *señorita* had dallied the night before, and on to cross the river.

He headed towards the Tarantula homestead. Suddenly he saw a cloud of dust aiming diagonally towards him which turned out to be cowboys heading in a bunch of wild horses. One detached himself and came riding across to confront him.

'What you doing here?' the cowboy shouted, and noticing Slaughter's well-worn apparel asked, 'You looking for work?'

'Maybe,' Slaughter replied, realizing that the Tarantula foreman had not recognized him from the day before. Well, there had been a lot of people there.

'Can you use that gun?' His questioner nodded at the Schofield. 'If so we might be interested.'

'You looking for cowpokes or fast guns?'

'You could say both.'

'Well, I don't lug the damn heavy thang around just for show,' the lieutenant drawled. 'You see that prairie lark perched on that post over yonder?' He whipped out the long-barrelled revolver, held it outstretched, eased back the hammer and fired one shot. The lark jumped for its life and flew off.

'You missed.'

Slaughter restrained the startled stallion, spun the gun on his trigger finger and stuck it back in its holster. 'I didn't intend to hit it. I ain't into killin' li'l larks. And I ain't wasting no more lead to prove some point to you.'

'That's proof enough.' The cowboy was short and wiry, in his mid-thirties. 'The handle's Frost. Tom Frost. Don't make a crack about Jack. I'm tired of hearing it. I'm the ramrodder of this outfit. C'm on, I'll take you to see the boss.'

The ranch house was just round a bend in the trail, not far from the line of hills. They followed the wranglers and their herd to the corrals and rode on to the imposing main building. It was a two-storey edifice, a flat-roofed adobe, but built like a small castle. Its bedrooms opened out on to verandas that gave shade to the pillared walkway beneath. It appeared extremely well-fortified.

'Mr Henderson,' Frost yelled, pushing through the main door and removing his hat. A maid in a mob cap, feather duster in hand, pointed them to the ornately furnished main dining room. 'Got a guy here we might be able to use.'

Henderson was reclining on a red-plush chaise longue, smoking a cheroot, a cup of coffee by his side. He put aside a newspaper he was reading and eyed Slaughter quizzically.

'He's pretty handy with a six-gun,' Frost enthused.

The rancher didn't reply for a while. As always, he looked like he was decked out for a funeral, in a black frock-coat with satin lapels, white shirt and boot-string tie, his stovepipe pants part-covering tooled leather black boots. He had one leg stuck up on the chaise, the other foot on the carpet. His cleanshaven face was cadaverous beneath neatly combed black hair, and his grey eyes were cold as he took a sip of coffee and surveyed them.

'You damn fool! This must be that bounty hunter I been hearing about. A Pinkerton man. Ain't that so, mister?'

He slowly got to his feet putting the coffee aside as Slaughter nodded. 'Guess that's me.'

'So, what you want poking your nose in here? You ain't looking for work, are you?'

'Who knows.' Slaughter shrugged. 'What I got to say is kinda private.'

'OK, Tom, you can go.' Henderson strode across to stand beneath a big oil painting of longhorns on the move beneath a cloudy sky. 'And shut the door after you.'

'Seems you've been informed why I'm here.'

'Sure, and I had nothing to do with that train robbery, so what do you want with me?'

'Well, it's like this. Seems like I ain't welcome in this vicinity. Pretty soon, I'm sure, there'll be an attempt to assassinate me. Maybe they'll succeed. So, all I want is to get this over with and hightail it back to Tucson 'fore they do. But I ain't leaving empty-handed, if you know what I mean.'

Henderson's thin lips twitched a faint smile. 'You think I know where that missing cash is? You want to do a deal? Is that it?'

'There's twenty-five thousand in bills still unaccounted for. Somebody must know where it is. Quite frankly, I couldn't give a damn whether the railroad or the banks get it back. All I want is my ten per cent.'

'You're joking?' This time the rancher really did crack a grin. 'I ain't a clue where the damn money is or who took it.'

'Yeah, tell that to the birds. Nice picture.' He nodded at the painting. 'Seems like I'm wasting my time so I'll say so long.'

'Hold your horses.' Henderson paced back to the chaise longue, turned on his heel and jabbed his cheroot at Slaughter. 'Let's say if, and that's a big if, I could locate whoever's got that cash. You're saying you want two thousand five hundred dollars of it, then you'll ride away and forget the whole thing, no names to nobody?'

'That's what I said. I'll simply tell Pinkerton I ran up against a brick wall and have given up on the case. No skin off my nose. I'm only temporarily on his payroll. I intend settling down and getting myself a nice big ranch like this.'

Slaughter himself gave a wide grin, partly because he wasn't sure whether he believed his own lies. Why, indeed, shouldn't he take such a course of action?

'That's the deal,' he said. 'Take it or leave it. But you can also warn whoever it is you're going to contact not to try tangling with me. I got a real itchy trigger finger these days. I don't want no monkey tricks.'

'I'll think about it,' Henderson stared at him as if he were trying to read his mind. 'I'll be in touch.'

He escorted Slaughter out and over to the corral where he had hitched the stallion.

The braggart Hans Groper was leaning against the top rail and beamed at him. 'You come to join our merry band?'

Slaughter glanced at him, noting the twin ivory-handled .45s pigstringed to his powerful thighs. 'You must be the dude who fancies himself a fast gun I've heard about.'

Groper leered at him, straightening up. 'Any time you want to roll the dice we'll roll the dice.'

'Yeah, I'll remember that.' The bounty hunter swung on to his stallion and nudged him away. '*Adios.*'

As they watched him go, Henderson touched Groper's arm.

'Kill him,' he said.

Aaron Snipe was sprawled on the widow's wonky brass bed wearing very little else but his bowler hat. Partly due to the curvature of the springs, and partly to her own amorous inclinations, the widow was rolled in close beside him.

'You're very quiet, Mr Fogerty.'

'Yeah, I'm thinking.'

'What of? Me, I hope.'

'Nope, that feller in the saloon, the bounty hunter. I don't go a lot on his chances. I heard some bozos say they were gonna get him. I wonder where he's gotten to?'

'What's that got to do with you?' She inveigled her icy fingers into his underpants. 'How's Big Willy today? Ooh dear, seems like he's little willy.'

'Yuh, he's taking a rest. You oughta lay off the cough medicine, Elspeth. It does funny thangs to you.'

'Come on,' she coaxed. 'You know your little friend wants to.'

'No.' Aaron leaped out of bed and pulled on his trousers. 'I gotta go.'

'No, Mr Fogerty,' she screeched, trying to catch hold of him. 'Don't leave me.'

'Don't fret, darling.' Snipe skipped away from her clutches. 'I'll be back . . . I hope.'

*

Slaughter had headed Henry up across a craggy range of hills with the idea that it might be a short cut back to town. But he had entered a steep-sided ravine that proved to be a dead-end. 'Come on boy,' he said, peering up at the cliff. 'There's no way we're getting up that. We better go back.'

That was his plan until the bullet took his hat off. He leapt from the stallion's back, pulling him into cover. 'Hot damn!' He ground-hitched him firmly to a rock. 'Stay there.' He leapt for another rock as a second bullet spurted into the dust and the report bounced off the ravine walls, echoing away. He levered his own carbine and aimed at the puff of smoke. It flushed out his assailant, a *hombre* in range clothes, who stepped forward firing what looked to be a 12-shot Winchester. Slaughter matched him with the Spencer's seven, pumping out lead as they marched towards each other.

'Got him!' the lieutenant breathed out as the man tumbled forwards, dropping the carbine, his hands groping desperately in the dust for life. But for him it was a lost battle.

Another rifle shot cracked out from the other side of the ravine and Slaughter spun round, cursing himself, for he should have known the bushwhacker would not have been alone. His Spencer was empty so he tossed it away, snatched out his revolver, but, before he could even cock it, looking up he saw the second assailant plough forwards into the dust, hit by a bullet in the back. His body rolled down towards Slaughter and lay still.

'Hell's bells!' Up on the ridge a third man on horse-back was silhouetted against the sun's flashing rays. He raised his rifle in casual, almost mocking salute to the man down in the ravine, turned and rode away. 'Who the devil's he?'

He looked down at Bob Olliphant whose upturned eyes, bulging like hard-boiled eggs, were unseeing. 'The deputy!' He climbed up the opposite cliff to identify his sidekick and, as expected, recognized a man who, during his beating in jail, he had heard called Joe.

'That other feller mighta saved our bacon,' he told Henry as he reloaded his carbine from his belt, 'but why didn't he hang around? Who was he?'

He reluctantly left the Winchester carbine where it lay. The latest model, it was an excellent saddle gun. But he didn't want to be accused of robbing the dead, or of being a back-shooter. For that reason he decided to leave the two bodies where they lay. To take the lawmen back into Visalia might be suicidal.

'I ain't buryin' the varmints, either.' He glanced up at the sky where turkey vultures were already circling, eager for their supper. It was odd that the gunshots had not brought anyone else to investigate. The Henderson ranch was not that far off.

'Let's git outa here 'fore anyone comes,' he said, swinging into the saddle. 'This canyon's giving me the creeps. It's just another dead end, like this whole darn case. We ain't gittin' nowhere, no how.'

It was getting dark in Visalia, which appeared to be as quiet as the grave. The stores were shuttered. A line of freight cars stood idle on the single track which headed away from the town in both directions, north and south, in long, straight, uncluttered lines. The customary sound of music and chatter from the saloons was muted.

'Where is everybody?' a wandering cowhand asked.

'Along at the town meeting,' was the reply.

Sure enough, a lot of hot air was emanating from inside the timber hall built alongside the white-painted church at the far end of town. Horses and buggies had been parked outside by farmers who had driven in from their smallholdings which were mostly cramped between the railroad and land owned by the ranchers.

'I'm sick and tired of their cattle rampaging over my crops,' a burly farmer complained. 'Why don't they put up wire to keep the damned stock where it belongs?'

The subject of barbed wire was a fiery topic thereabouts for cattlemen still believed in their right to the open range. The cowboy and the farmer always would be at loggerheads.

'Why don't you put up your own fences,' Hilarius Bogbinder asked, 'if it worries you so much?'

He was seated alongside the mayor and a couple of other town bigwigs on a raised platform. He stroked his pencil moustache with a little finger, giving his conceited smile.

'You any idea how much it would cost me to fence my land?' the farmer replied. 'You any idea how hard it is to make a living from a smallholding? We need every cent we can make.'

'That ain't the point,' another man butted in. 'Most of us are homesteaders. We were given our acres by the government. Most of us are making a living, fair enough. But, what we want to know is why can't we extend our holdings further out on to the free range? If that soil was properly turned we could grow some fine fruit and crops. It's wasted on cattle. Most of us would be willing to pay cash or take out a mortgage to extend our land. I thought that that was what this meeting was about.'

In the flickering oil lamps the faces of the audience, men and women in their shabby homespun, seemed to be etched with the rugged lines of hard work and anxiety. 'Yeah,' another shouted. 'Why should those dagoes have all that free land just because it was theirn 'fore the state was born? They got to abide by our laws now.'

This elicited a roar of approval from the crowd. White Anglo-Saxon protestants, as most of them were, if poor ones, had little fondness for their Latino Roman Catholic neighbours.

'Yes, that is the reason for this meeting,' the mayor cried out. 'To test the feelings of the citizens and to make application to the state legislature to extend your holdings. But it will all have to be done in a lawful manner; that is why Mr Bogbinder is here to advise.'

Sheriff Loomis rose to say, 'There is to be a court case next month when Don Miguel de Estudillo Puyol, as he grandly calls himself, will be summoned to prove what right he has to his land. I'm confident Judge Dixon will be sympathetic to the farmers, so I don't see what you're all gettin' so het up about.'

'We can't prejudge the case,' Bogbinder put in, 'but I too feel—'

Just then the door banged open and Henderson, in his funereal clothes and black, flat-topped hat, strutted down the aisle. 'We need Sheriff Loomis pretty quick. I got two of his deputies outside and they've both been shot dead,' he said.

The storeholders, townspeople and homesteaders clattered back their chairs and stomped noisily outside to take a look. 'Poor old Bob,' Loomis shouted, pointing to Olliphant. 'He's been shot in the back. He was a family man who served this town well. He didn't deserve this.'

'Joe Thornton's been backshot, too.' Henderson pointed to the wound in the corpse hanging over his mustang's saddle. 'We heard gunshots coming from a ravine in the hills and when we got there we found these two dead. Another man was riding away. A man on a big stallion.'

'Who was he?' a woman screamed. 'The swine. He musta shot these boys down in cold blood.'

'Who do you think?' Henderson scowled. 'That bounty hunter who's been sniffing around.'

'That half-breed Indian called Slaughter,' the sheriff roared. 'I told the judge that man was a mad dog killer and would kill again if he let him go. He wouldn't have it, said there was no case. Well, we got a case now. The sooner we catch him and hang him the better it will be for everybody in this neighbourhood.'

'Are you sure about this?' Aaron Snipe quavered anxiously. 'I mean have you any proof it was him? They mighta been trying to kill him. It mighta been self-defence.'

'Of course it was him,' Henderson shouted. 'Earlier he had the nerve to call in on me at my ranch and made slanderous accusations that I had something to do with that train robbery. He even tried to bribe me, saying if I paid him two and a half thousand dollars he'd go away and forget about it. What kinda Pinkerton man is that? A damned crooked one. I informed him in no uncertain terms that I knew nothing about the robbery and told him to get lost.'

'That lousy, two-bit southern Reb,' Loomis sneered. 'Which way was he headed, Mr Henderson?'

'Towards Don Miguel's ranch. I hear he's become quite a pal of theirn.'

'Right,' the sheriff hollered. 'Any of you men willing to join my posse go home and get your guns. We'll congregate outside the saloon at midnight and ride to Don Miguel's to smoke the rat out of his hole.'

NINE

The white-garbed riders were pounding up and down Visalia's main drag, two of them brandishing flaming oil brands in their hands. In their Ku Klux Klan-style robes they looked eerily merciless and most of the citizenry had locked themselves away behind their doors.

'Ain't anybody else gonna join us?' their leader yelled, his eyes and lips glistening threateningly through the slits in his mask. 'What's the matter with you cowards? We vigilantes are riding to seek vengeance on the murderer of two good deputies and them that helped him.'

But many of the farmers and storekeepers who had responded eagerly to the call at the meeting had had a change of heart, especially when they saw the way it was to be. Others' wives had browbeaten them not to risk their lives, for the sake of their children. And numerous of the town population were suffering from severe diarrhoea, no doubt due to over-imbibing the carpetbagger's bellyache aniseed, or possibly from swallowing the oil of earthworms instead of rubbing it into the skin.

Indeed, there were mutterings that Aaron ought to be

tarred and feathered and run out of town dangling from a pole.

'I cannot countenance this,' Sheriff Loomis shouted, standing outside his office. 'I called for supporters of a lawful posse, not vigilantes.'

'So stay behind, yeller-belly!' yelled a stout rider, wearing a brace of ivory-handled pistols buckled around his waist. The voice was obviously Hans Groper's behind his hood. 'Let's go get 'em, boys.'

'Right,' the leader shouted. 'We'll do the sheriff's work for him. Follow me.'

With that he and his followers went surging out of the main street, heading out on to the moonlit plain, riding hard.

'Let them go, Trick,' Bogbinder advised. 'There's more than one way of killing a cat. Better that they should get the blame rather than you. There's election time coming up.'

'All right, you others,' the sheriff shouted. 'You can all go home.'

He headed with Bogbinder for the saloon.

It was gone midnight by the time the vigilantes reached the Laguna prairie. They paused before riding in to the hacienda to light more tar brands and check their weapons.

'Shoot to kill,' the leader shouted. 'It's time we wiped out these greaser rats.'

They were a terrifying sight for the Mexican women and children and the Indian servants as they charged in in their ghostly costumes, hurling their brands at the flat roofs of the low-lying hacienda buildings.

But the *vaqueros* were ready for them, armed and dangerous, hiding on those rooftops, tossing the brands back at the horsemen as they galloped by, making their horses rear and scream with fright.

Others were in place behind a barricade of wagons that had been hauled across the entrance to the hacienda at the suggestion of Slaughter that afternoon. When he had arrived he told the *ranchero* that he had been set up as the killer of the two deputies and said he had a hunch a posse would attack using the deaths of the deputies as an exscuse.

So the battle was vicious, violent and short-lived as a hail of lead met the attackers in the night. Several of the vigilantes cartwheeled from their saddles as their mustangs crashed, writhing, to the ground.

'We've turned the tables on them, men,' Don Miguel cried. 'They did not expect this. Show them how a Mexican fights. Meet fire with fire!'

The women behind them were busy reloading rifles and pistols, tossing them up to the snipers on the roofs. Black powder smoke billowed. The night was rent with screams and shouts and moans of the the wounded.

'They've set the stables alight,' Ricardo shouted.

'We must save the horses,' Don Miguel replied. 'Go get them, *muchachos*.'

His *vaqueros* leapt without hesitation over the barricades and surged out, firing at the white-garbed riders while running to rescue the stock. They fought their way into the big stable which was billowing smoke, its hay catching fast. They caught hold of the whinnying beasts,

103

released them from their stalls and dragged them out to safety.

Their attackers had had enough, but as Slaughter brought Raquel's gelding and Ricardo's Arab mare from the stable one of them charged his mustang at him, his revolver aimed point blank to shoot him down. Before he could do so one of his companions in Ku Klux Klan garb whirled his mustang around and put a bullet into the assailant's side, tumbling him from the saddle.

Caught off guard Slaughter looked with surprise at the one who had saved him. The little vigilante appeared to grin from behind his mask, and gave the thumbs up sign. He swirled his mustang around, then seeing that the rest of his gang had fled, pulled off his mask.

'Aaron, you weasel, what are you doing here?'

'Earning my pay,' Snipe replied, holstering his revolver. 'Which reminds me, you owe me another week's.'

They left the Mexicans to care for their injured and try to douse the stable fire, and sauntered back to the hacienda courtyard where Doña Puyol was screaming from her window, 'Kill the Antichrist! Kill them all!'

'Watch out for the bloodthirsty old biddy,' Slaughter remarked. 'She's inclined to dump her pisspot on your head.'

More shots were ringing out beyond the walls and they knew the *vaqueros* would be giving the *coup de grâce* with relish to the enemy injured. They took no prisoners.

Raquel appeared to be hysterical too, coming from the house, screaming at him, 'You are the cause of all this? Why did you come here bringing all this torment and death?'

'If the gringo had not come to warn us,' Don Miguel pointed out, 'we would all have been murdered in our beds.'

'Mr Henderson is not like that,' she sobbed. 'He only wanted him caught and hanged.'

'You seem pretty sure it was Henderson behind this,' Slaughter drawled. 'By the way I got your horse out safe. No need for thanks.'

'Yes, Daughter,' Don Miguel probed. 'How do you know so much about Henderson? What is going on?'

'Oh, you silly old man. You live in the past,' she screamed. 'Why don't you leave me alone?' She flounced back into the house.

Slaughter grinned at Don Miguel. 'Ain't easy having a daughter, huh?'

It was midnight the following day when Slaughter rode his stallion into Visalia, hoping that he was unseen, and made his way by the backstreets to the Mexican quarter. He hung around in the shadows outside the Devil's Cauldron until the last few customers seemed to have left and Anna appeared, closing the wooden doors after them, calling out, '*Buenos noches, señores.*'

Slaughter strolled over, put a foot in the door before she shut it. 'Hi,' he said, 'how about a drink?'

'No, it is late. Come back tomorrow.'

'Aw, I got a terrible hankering for one of them lime-juice tequilas.'

'As long as that's all you've got a hankering for.' She

105

smiled at him and appeared to change her mind. 'Come on in.'

'You're a sweetheart.'

Anna's hips swayed in the peasant skirt as she went behind the bar and as she reached for the bottle he admired the enticing shadowy valley between her breasts cupped in the off-the-shoulder blouse.

'Guess you heard about the shindig out at the *rancho*. A dozen men gunned down. I've an idea I'm *persona non grata* in this town.'

She shrugged and handed him his drink. 'It is no concern of mine. I just run this bar. Men are such fools.'

'Yeah, that's true. Allus fighting. Me, I'm passionately dedicated to peace and pleasure.'

'Really?' She laughed, tossing back her luxuriant black hair. 'That's nice.' She filled a glass with iced white wine and toasted him. 'Here's to peace and pleasure.'

'Heard tell you were pally with the sheriff. Now that feller *is* a fool.'

'Oh, I wouldn't say that. But it was a long time ago. It is all over now.'

'Why so?'

'He was OK at first. But when he wanted to move in with me and take fifty per cent of all I make I gave him his marching orders. Nobody owns me.'

'Good girl. I wouldn't want to follow in his footsteps, but I guess if it's all over it's OK.'

'What do you mean?'

'Well, you said yourself it's getting late.' He appraised her hour-glass figure, her arrogant stance. 'Bedtime.'

'You've got a nerve,' she said in Spanish. 'You think

you can just come in here?'

'Aw, come on, honey.' He slapped a dollar coin down for the drinks. 'What's the night and a bed for? Why waste it?'

Her dark eyes appeared hesitant as she surveyed him. 'Why, indeed!' She came around the bar and bolted the door. He caught her around the waist as she returned and pulled her tight into him. Her body was warm and sinuous, her tongue slipping between his lips as they kissed. She pointed to a back room when the kissing ceased. 'It's in there. The bed, I mean. I'll just tidy up in here. Go on, relax.'

She collected the glasses as he did as she bid. It was a simply furnished room. A glass-topped door was open to a back patio to let in the night air. He looked out at a walled garden. No problem. He unbuckled his gunbelt, hung it from the bed post and lay on his back putting his moccasin boots up, his hat over his nose.

Anna laughed when she saw him. 'You're a cool customer.'

He examined the bullet hole in his hat, and tossed it into a corner and pulled her on top of him. 'And you're a hot one,' he hissed as she straddled him. 'A real hot number. Don't it worry you having a killer in your bed? They say I gunned down them two deputies.' For answer she pulled off her blouse to expose her magnificent melon breasts, their erect nipples in dark aureolas. She made them tremble as she shook out her black mane of hair.

'No, it doesn't. You excite me.'

'Good.' He craned forward to kiss her again, from her

107

loose lips to her breasts and down to her belly-button, licking at her as if relishing the feast. ' 'Cause you do the same to me.'

Anna glanced at a gold watch hanging from a nail on the wall and murmured, 'Yes, that is obvious. Don't be in such a hurry. Take your time. We have all night. Let me see.' She jerked down his pants to expose him. 'Mmm. What a big boy.'

What she did to him next Slaughter could only describe as heavenly bliss. But soon he could take no more, rolling her over on to her back, pulling up her skirt, thrusting into her as she ran her fingernails down his back and all else was forgotten. She was moaning and groaning and holding him so tight he didn't hear the boot-step as a man came through the door from the patio. But he froze when he heard the words.

'Get outa that woman, you lowdown skunk.'

Slaughter turned to see Sheriff Loomis and looked into the deathly hole of his Peacemaker. Had he held fire for fear a .45 slug would penetrate the two of them at such close range?

'Aw, Sheriff,' he complained. 'Cain't you see you're interrupting?'

Then from the corner of his eye he saw Anna bringing out her stiletto from under the mattress, swinging it to lunge at his jugular. He caught her wrist, twisted it from her, rolled out of the bed as Loomis fired. The explosion racketed out and the bullet blasted into her. Down on his knees, he hurled the knife and it thudded into the sheriff's chest.

Slaughter grabbed his Schofield, thumbing the

hammer. But he did not need to fire. Loomis fell forward, eyes bulging with disbelief, gasping like a hooked fish, and collapsed on to Anna.

The lieutenant backed away, staring at the two bodies as the blood pooled from them on to the bedclothes. Anna's eyes were staring at him. They had lost their warm glow. 'Jeez!' he whistled.

He pulled up his pants, found his shirt and hat, buckled on the gun, pulled out the stiletto and put it into her hand, wrapping her fingers around it. 'Looks like one of them lovers' quarrels,' he muttered. 'Rest in peace, sweetheart.'

He went out into the bar, poured himself another drink. 'Hell, ain't I ever gonna get some proper lovin' in this town?' he mused. 'I was nearly done.' He noticed the bell-pull cord hanging down. It was probably connected to the sheriff's office a hundred yards away. She had summoned him. And her own death.

There were sounds of voices from outside. Somebody was hammering at the door. He went back into the bedroom to the man sprawled on the naked woman. He pulled Loomis back, got hold of her wrist and shoved the stiletto deep into him up to the handle. On an afterthought he ripped Trick's shirt and trousers open as if they might have been having sex. He took a ring of keys from the sheriff's belt; his fingers were already tightened around the grip of the revolver so Slaughter left it as it was.

'Right,' he muttered. 'Now to take a look in his office.' The door was splintering open as he slipped into the back yard and vaulted over the wall into an alley. All in a day's work, he thought. Wonder what I can charge for expenses?

He could hear a commotion going on along at the Devil's Cauldron. He unlocked the jailhouse door and stepped inside. The one remaining deputy must have gone along to investigate.

'What's happening?' some drunk wailed from a cell along the corridor.

'Ah, shuddup,' growled Slaughter. He went through the desk drawers but there was nothing of significance. He unlocked the big safe, swung the door open and was rewarded by the sight of a pile of cash. He struck a match, shielding it with one hand as he examined the serial numbers of the notes. None matched the stolen bills. He looked in a cash-box. Just coin. He searched through other documents but drew a blank. If Trick Loomis had been involved in the robbery he must have hidden the loot someplace else, but Slaughter was beginning to doubt if he had been.

He was going to leave the bundle of notes, about $500, in the safe as he shut it, but changed his mind and stuffed it into the pocket of his leather coat. 'The sheriff's ill-gotten gains ain't gonna be any good to him now,' he muttered, glancing at a row of bells on the wall, which were no doubt connected by pulleys to the bank and saloons. 'I deserve some compensation from them two fer tryin' to murder me.'

All was quiet outside as he locked up and went a few doors along the sidewalk to Hilarius Bogbinder's law office. A lantern was glowing inside. He hammered on the door.

'Who's there?' a voice from inside called.

'It's me, the mayor,' Slaughter squawked, and, as the door was unlocked and Bogbinder poked his head out, he rabbit-punched him hard from one side to the back of his neck, then caught the lawyer as he collapsed and dragged him back inside.

He dumped him on the floor and took a look around. There were files for this, that and the other everywhere. Slaughter didn't waste time. He swept them aside and made a hurried search for a hiding-place, tossing boxes and red-ribboned court files on to the floor.

'What's going on?' Bogbinder murmured as he stirred, almost buried by his own workload.

It crossed Slaughter's mind to question him, force him to tell him all he knew, but he doubted if that would work, so he buffaloed him again. 'You can shut up, too.'

He found his keys and opened his safe. Again no sign of the missing cash. Maybe it *was* in the bank.

Slaughter stood and stroked his chin, somewhat exasperated. He seemed to be no nearer solving the case unless Ricardo was right and the late sheriff and his gimcrack lawyer had it salted away. But he somehow doubted that.

He locked the safe and the office door behind him, put the keys in his pocket.

'Now where did I leave that damned horse?' he asked himself as he headed away through the quiet streets.

TEN

'Howdy, Loo-tenant.' Aaron Snipe poked his head out of the widow's bedroom window. 'What you want this time of night?'

'I want you to catch the first train to Bakersfield, then head for Los Angeles puebla. It's on the coast. Find this woman.' Slaughter stood in the stirrups and handed up a name scrawled on a bit of paper. 'Put that in your shirt pocket. Don't lose it.'

'Hang on.' Snipe ducked back in to the cottage bedroom, then poked his head back through the curtains. 'She says there ain't no train 'til eight a.m.'

'Be on it. This is important. Here.' He tossed Snipe a bankroll of one hundred dollars. 'It's a bonus from the late sheriff. Don't spend it on booze. I want you back in at least two days' time.'

'You got my word, Loo-tenant. I'm keeping on the straight and narrow. So what you want me to find out from this lady?'

'Exactly where she got that fifty dollar bill from – the one from the train robbery – and don't take any guff about she got it from some gambling man. You get my drift?'

'Sure, I'll git it out of her. So – uh – whadda ya mean, *late* sheriff? You gone an' killed him?'

'Aaron, you know I don't kill nobody unless they try to kill me.'

A voice from inside the bedroom wailed, 'Mr Fogerty, who are you talking to? Come to bed.'

'Some stranger wants to know the time of the trains. Keep your engine running, Elspeth,' he called back to her, then winked at his former lieutenant. 'I gotta go. She's got the old kitchen kettle on the boil and it's about to whistle.'

'OK. I figure I'd best make myself scarce for a coupla days. You recall them cabins down on the lake? I'm gonna do me a spot of fishing. You can find me there.'

'Right, will do.' Aaron saluted. 'Goodnight, suh!'

'Goodnight to you, too, Corporal.' Slaughter grinned in the moonlight and nudged the stallion away. 'Take it easy,' he called, and put his big horse into a fast gallop away from the town.

He got a few hours shut-eye laid out on his saddle and blanket in the shade of one of the big oaks on the Laguna spread, hoping that the big old grizzly didn't happen by. However, as he was carrying no food he felt reasonably safe with his Spencer carbine held between his knees.

Later in the morning he was riding towards Don Miguel's ranch house when Ricardo appeared on his fine white mare, a bunch of men by his side.

'What do you want?' demanded the young man.

'I got somethang for your father.'

'I will give it him,' Ricardo said, holding out his hand.

'I'd rather give it him myself.'

'Don't trust him,' Raoul, the scar-faced *mayordomo* spat out. 'He is an *Americano*. They are all snakes in the grass.'

'Aw, come on. I did my share of the fighting to help protect your ranch the other night. Me and my pal potted two of those guys.'

'This man is as crafty as a prairie fox,' Raoul insisted. 'I am warning you, Ricardo, you cannot trust him.'

'Waal, it looks like I'm kinda in no man's land, don't it? The *Americanos* want me dead. And you boys don't trust me. So I guess I'd better ride on alone.'

'Just a minute,' Ricardo called. 'I will take you to see my father. We will see what it is you have for him.'

'Whoa, boy,' Slaughter shouted, trying to control his randy stallion. 'I better get him up ahead of your mare.'

As he did so Raoul hissed at Ricardo: 'You are a fool. Kill him now. Have done with it. This man is trouble. I can read it in his eyes.'

'All *Americanos* are trouble,' Ricardo replied. 'This one has been useful to us. I think it best to keep him on our side for the moment.' He touched his golden spurs to the mare. 'Come on, let's go.'

'So,' Don Miguel asked, studying the legal documents Slaughter had tossed on to his desk. 'Henderson is claiming twenty thousand acres of my land. Where did you get this?'

'I happened to notice it when I was searching through

114

the lawyer's stuff last night.' Slaughter grinned. 'Illegally I might add. Bogbinder was in the land of Nod at the time. He will be appearing for Henderson at the county court you've been summoned to. This is his complete plan of campaign. I'd strongly advise you to show it to a lawyer of your own.'

'This is too much,' the old man roared. 'He tried to take my land by force of arms in the middle of the night and we gave him a bloody nose. It is time we showed this upstart wolf just who he is dealing with.'

'I wouldn't be too hasty. He's still got some tasty gunmen in his mob. You were lucky the other night.'

'Rubbish. We have ruled the prairies for three centuries. I will send my *mayordomo* to recruit *compañeros* from our neighbours. We will wipe Henderson from the face of the map.'

'Waal, I don't know about that,' Slaughter said with a sigh.

'I do know. And you, my friend, I hope will stay to join us.'

The bounty hunter scratched at his thick black thatch with exasperation. 'My days as a mercenary are over. First, tomorrow, I gotta go down to the hunters' cabins to meet my pal. I'll see what he has to say. We might look like a couple of knaves but to tell you the truth we both try to do what we think is the right thing.'

'So, what's your problem?' Don Miguel cried. 'We have right on our side.'

'Well.' Slaughter smiled, 'We'll see.'

Outside he met Raquel, just returned from her horse ride. Her eyes flashed with anger. 'What do you want here? To stir up more trouble for us?'

'No, I've just been invited to stay the night. Maybe we could git together later, if you ain't got nothin' else to do.'

'What? You must be joking. What's the matter? Why can't you find yourself a common woman of the town?'

'Wall, I did,' he drawled,' but it was kinda *coitus* very much *interruptus*. What you might call an unfinished symphony.'

'Ha!' Raquel snorted contemptuously and pushed past him.

Slaughter watched her go. 'She's sure got a nice *derrière*,' he mused, sticking a hand in his pants to untangle himself. 'Down, boy. Don't think we're welcome in that department.'

At Bakersfield there was much talk of a new railroad to be built to Los Angeles, but it was yet to be completed. So Aaron was tossed back and forth inside a stagecoach that made the hundred-mile journey across the Tehachapi mountains.

It was late afternoon by the time they rolled in, after three changes of horses, to the small, sleepy market town set amid orange groves and vineyards. There was one main mud-hard street with a variety of stores, warehouses and saloons. Dusty trails led off to other houses and farmsteads. In the war it had been a stronghold of Southern men, mostly Missourians. Those who had settled here were not noted for their industry, more for their love of the bottle. So Aaron was in his element as he bought a round or two and soon discovered that Helga

Bjorn, a lady of Swedish descent, lived in the old village.

The original puebla, with its defensive, adobe-walled courtyard, had been founded in 1781 by Felipe de Neve. The clangour of the mission bell summoned the Catholic faithful as he found her house in the old town, a twenty-feet high bougainvillaea trailing over its walls. Once it must have been splendid but now everything, like the garden, had fallen into ruin and decay. The garden gate creaked open, and Aaron went through the bushes to a piazza, where he saw a leggy ash-blonde sprawled, half-dressed, on a hammock.

'Yeah?' she called. 'What you sellin'? Before you start your spiel I don' need none.'

Aaron guessed that in his suit and bowler he must look like a hawker so he tried to give a severe frown and said, 'I ain't sellin' nuthin', ma'am. Ahm a federal investigator here to ask you a few questions.'

'Aw, get lost.' She was about fifty. Her classical Nordic features showed she had once been beautiful. Alas, the ravages of time, gravity, alcohol and dissipation had taken their toll on her face and body. 'Who do you think you are? What right you got to come walking in here?'

She made no attempt to cover her still-shapely legs: strange in a town when most of the females were smothered in skirts past their ankles, high-buttoned blouses and floppy sunhats.

'I got every right. The county sheriff, or whoever runs this town, mighta got you off the hook six months ago, but this time you're for the high jump unless you co-operate.'

'You're in my sun,' she replied dismissively, regally

waving him away with a hand holding a glass of tequila, a cigarette between the fingers. 'We've been through all that. Case dismissed.'

'Sun?' Aaron noticed her fingers trembled in spite of her bravado, and her speech was slurred.

'Yes, it's good for you.'

'First I've heard of it. Anyhow, unless you start talkin', sister, you're looking at a two-year stretch in San Quentin. Who gave you that stolen fifty? Was it Don Miguel de Estudillo Puyol? It's common knowledge you were his mistress for twenty years. Some fellas along at the saloon just told me so.'

'Sure, he had the best of me and then, since fallin' off his damn horse, he ain't been this way in seven years.'

'But he still sends you gifts from time to time?'

'Huh! Time to time. You've got it. He shoulda divorced that crazy religious bitch and married me if he had any decency. He stole my daughter and when do I see her? Once in a blue moon.'

'So, who gave you the fifty? Him or her?'

'Leave me alone,' she groaned, sitting up unsteadyily in the hammock and reaching for the almost empty bottle to splash the remains in her glass.

'Listen.' Aaron produced an unopened bottle of tequila from his bag and waggled it before her. 'I'm warning you. I could have you arrested now. Or I could leave you this and be on my way.'

'Ach.' With a guttural cry she reached for the bottle, but he held it back from her. 'Please, just a drop.'

'Which is it to be?'

'All right, Raquel gave it to me, but she didn't know it

was stolen. Neither did I.'

'That's all I wanted to know.' He tossed the bottle to her. 'So long.'

Snipe didn't look back. With any luck he could catch the overnight stage back to Bakersfield, and the next train to Visalia, pick up his buckskin nag from Elspeth's cottage and find James Slaughter by noon tomorrow.

'Sold her daughter down the river for a bottle of booze,' he muttered. 'That's how the licker gats ya. I gotta stay on the water wagon from here on.'

The next day, late afternoon, Slaughter was sitting on the rickety jetty at the lake watching a raccoon that had climbed out on to the tula reeds and was hanging down precariously trying to catch one of the numerous fish swimming below. 'He's gonna come a cropper if he don't watch out.'

Some hunters on horseback had arrived, so he went up to see if he could glean any news. Elijah, the 'keep, had given him a very sullen welcome on his return but had reluctantly provided him with a plate of gooseleg in gravy. Now he was serving the hunters, who were busy discussing the latest events detailed in the *Visalia Plainspeaker* which one of them had brought with him.

'RANGE WAR ERUPTS,' ran the banner headline. 'TWELVE MEN DEAD.' A cross-head said, 'REVENGE ATTACKS EXPECTED.'

'Don Miguel's boys were ready for them vigilantes,' one of the hunters remarked. 'They kilt eight of 'em. Two of them was farmers and t'others turned out to be Henderson's gunmen.'

'So both sides are gonna be seething like hives of disturbed bees to git at each other's throats agin,' another man yelled, as he imbibed a tumbler of Moonface's moonshine.

'I see the mayor's calling for the state military to intervene,' the first hunter muttered. 'Ain't much chance of that. Best to wait and watch 'em wipe each other out.'

'SHERIFF STABBED TO DEATH BY HIS LOVER,' the other main front page story announced.

'He got what was coming to him,' one of the shabby coves at the far end of the bar sneered. 'He shoulda known better than to tangle with that fiery Mex bitch Anna Matiz.'

'Looks like Loomis shot her then fell on top of her when she put her pig-sticker in his heart,' a hunter remarked. 'Or t'other way round. Maybe she stuck him first. Hang on, it says here some witness claims to have seen another man leaving over the back wall shortly after the gun shot alerted folks.'

'Funny that lawyer's office was broke into at the same time,' another man said, pointing to another story. 'Says he got robbed of five thousand dollars.'

'Five thou'?' Slaughter exploded. 'Damn lyin' bastard.'

The bar room fell silent as they all turned to give him the once-over, suspicion in their eyes.

'Waal, you know what they're like,' he defended himself. 'Lawyers, huh! I would bet that safe was empty.'

'You seem to know a lot about it,' Moonface accused.

'That guy's a jerk. His picture's in the dictionary next to the word. Gimme a beer, will ya?'

He was sitting on a barrel supping his beer when the Laguna ranch *mayordomo* pushed into the bar. 'What you doing here?' the scar-faced Raoul snarled when he saw him. 'You hiding out? Running scared of a lynch party from Visalia getting you?'

Slaughter rose to his feet, put the glass aside and faced him. 'I sometimes get the feeling you don't like me. Who are your new sweethearts?'

Raoul had three hard-faced *vaqueros* beside him. They were holding rifles and were draped with bandoleers of bullets. 'I've been raising reinforcements.'

'Don't look like you've had much success.'

'Ach! That cowardly General Beale, he did not want to know.'

'Can't say I blame him. You planning on starting a new Mex war aginst the states?'

'Get out of my way.' Raoul pushed past him to get to the bar. 'This man stabbed the sheriff,' he shouted, 'and killed Anna Matiz, too.'

'Not so fast.' Slaughter caught hold of his shirt, tearing it back from his chest to reveal the deep white scar of a recent wound. 'I thought as much. It was you.'

Raoul backed away. 'Keep your hands off me. For your information I got this wound years ago. I was gored by a bull.'

'Yeah, blabbermouth? Tell that to the bees. Or to a jury.'

The hunters scrambled to clear a space as the three *vaqueros* fanned out beside Raoul, their hands hovering over their gun-grips, grins spreading over their faces, knowing the advantage was theirs, four to one. 'Come

121

on, gringo,' one coaxed. 'Go for it.'

Slaughter faced them. His gunbelt wasn't aligned as he liked but he didn't dare touch it. 'I would advise you three men to get out of here,' he gritted out. 'This ain't your quarrel. It's 'tween me and him.'

When they didn't make a move, just stood there leering at him, he backed away. 'I'm giving you this chance to surrender, Raoul. You can say your piece in court.'

Raoul's eyes flashed and he was the first to go for his gun, the other's following suit. There was a cracking of shots as Slaughter's right hand whipped the Texan Schofield from its greased holster faster than the eye could follow, gritting his teeth, fanning the hammer until the cylinder was empty. Two of the *vaqueros* were hit before they cleared their irons from their belts and were hurled back against the wall; there was the flash of an explosion from the open door and Raoul spun on his bootheels as the lead smashed through his side, his ribcage and heart. It came out the other side, sending him teetering back against the bar. The third *vaquero* got his shot away, but missed Slaughter by a fraction, the slug tearing through his shirtsleeve. Slaughter's bullet put the Mexican down. Raoul was leaning back on the bar trying to raise his revolver, his face agonized as blood spurted from his shirt. Aaron stepped through the door and finished him. His shot took off half of Raoul's skull and splattered Moonface with blood.

'Looks like I got here just in time,' Aaron said, with a grin.

'I coulda taken 'em all,' Slaughter muttered, as the

powder smoke wreathed him.

'I doubt it, Loo-tenant. Not even you coulda done that.'

It had all happened in the space of a few seconds. Suddenly the goose-hunters came back to life.

'I never thought to see Raoul Franco outgunned,' one remarked, gruffly.

'Franco? Was that his name?' Slaughter glanced at Aaron. 'Frank, they said he was called. The young one's voice was probably muffled by the mask.'

'The young one,' Snipe joined in. 'It could have been a gal. I'm thinking Raquel. She passed that fifty-dollar bill from the robbery to her mother.'

'Yep, and the third robber was her brother, Ricardo. Where else did he get the cash to buy gold spurs and saddle horn?'

'So,' Aaron wondered, as he kicked at the corpses to make sure they were dead, 'who was the brains behind the outfit? Who's holding those twenty-five thousand greenbacks? Don Miguel? The lawyer? Or was it the sheriff?'

Suddenly it had all become clear to Slaughter, everything swinging into place. 'No, the old man had nothing to do with it. The lawyer and the sheriff were simply in Henderson's pay with orders to get rid of any nosy Pinkerton men. It's Henderson who's pulled the strings and got the judge running scared, I'm pretty sure of that. He's the man we got to see. Come on, we got to ride.'

'Aw, hold on, Loo-tenant, I've just rode fifty miles. I need a sup of that whiskey 'fore it's all gone.' Aaron nodded at the bullet-holed barrel which was spouting moonshine. 'And a fresh horse.'

'All right,' Slaughter said. 'I'll give you ten minutes. There's four broncos hitched outside, these poor fools rode. Take your pick.'

ELEVEN

Raquel's corn-coloured hair was blowing wildly in the wind as, hatless, she whipped her fine gelding out from the Laguna hacienda. Her skirt billowing, it looked as if she were flying as she galloped the horse away across the prairie.

'Stop her!' Don Miguel's gravelly voice rasped out as he was helped from the house by his servants. 'She's going to warn him.'

But it was too late. Raquel was already just a speck on the horizon. 'Damn that girl. She's too much like her mother. It's her bad seed been passed on. How could she talk to me that way? That swine must have bewitched her, turned her against me.'

There had been a terrible argument that afternoon after the duenna had informed him, as her duty, that his daughter had been seduced by Henderson; that, unknown to her, she had been meeting him secretly, sneaking out at midnight when her chaperon was asleep.

'Yes,' Raquel had screamed when Don Miguel confronted her. 'I am going to marry him. Your day is over,

Father. You are a fool. Soon these government lands will be thrown open for settlement and Jack will buy you out. All this will be ours.'

'Jack? Is that what you call that rattlesnake?' Her father was choking on his anger. 'Go to your room. I'll soon settle Jack's problem. Tomas, get me my guns. Saddle my horse.'

'No!' Raquel shrieked. 'You can't. You will ruin everything.'

'It is you who are ruined. You think Henderson will marry you? When he has used you he'll cast you aside like a soiled rag. Take her to her room. Lock her up.'

'No!' She screamed some more as two of his house servants grabbed hold of her and dragged her away. 'Get off me! You can't do this.'

But then there was a commotion. Somehow she had escaped, raced to the stables where her horse had been saddled ready for her evening ride. Raquel had leapt into the saddle and whipped him away.

Ricardo stood uneasily, seeing his share of the 25,000 dollars fast disappearing, undecided what to do. He daren't reveal to his father how Henderson had masterminded the plan, inveigled Raqel into it, then him, too, while he, for his part, had recruited Raoul Franco, the only other conspirator. Nor dare he explain how Henderson had refused to part with the greenbacks, saying they must 'bide their time'. The gold coin he gave them hadn't lasted long.

'Father,' he asked sharply, 'what are you going to do?'

'Do?' the old man roared, breaking and loading the shotgun Tomas gave him. 'Henderson will find out what

I am going to do.'

He snapped the twelve-gauge double-barrel shut and struggled to his feet. 'Tomas, pass me my pistols. Tell the men to arm themselves. We are going to ride!'

Snipe had quickly tumbled off the proposed water wagon. One chipped mug full of sheepherders' delight was fast swallowed. 'Whoo!' With a shake of his head he was waggling his cup for a refill from the barrel.

'What do you put in this stuff?'

'Aw,' Moonface replied, 'I gen'rally toss my soiled long johns and worn socks in the brew and give it a stir. Gives it nice colour and adds to the bouquet.'

His Indians were busy dragging out the corpses of the *vaqueros* after he had claimed their weapons, bullets and boots. 'You can squabble 'mong yerselves for anything they got on 'em,' he called. 'Never do have nuthin' on 'em,' he said, with a wink. 'Spend it as fast as they git it.'

'You wanna watch out for that stuff,' one of the hunters advised Aaron. 'T'other night one of our boys got so drunk he crept up on his camp and stole his own bundle and gun, hid 'em in the woods, wandered off, slept under a bush, and in the marnin' complained that he'd been robbed. He never did find his stuff agin.'

The ten minutes had stretched into half an hour before Slaughter stormed in, grabbed Snipe by the scruff of the neck and marched him out to general applause.

'Come on. Git on a horse.'

Snipe did a double somersault, gave a rebel yell, tried to carry on the momentum and land on a horse but slithered over the other side instead. He eventually managed to get a foot in a stirrup and himself on its back and went zigzagging away.

'Damn crow-hopping buckskin,' he yelled. 'Bring my saddle-bags, Loo-tenant. I got a present for ya.'

After thirty miles of going at a steady lope he had just about sobered up and they soon drew in sight of the Laguna ranch house.

'What in hell's going on?' Slaughter shouted, as a wild, whooping band of sombreroed *vaqueros*, most brandishing carbines or rifles, came galloping out, led by Ricardo and Don Miguel, and wheeled away in the direction of the Tarantula spread.

'Looks like war's broke out,' Aaron yelled back. 'I need a change of horse if we're going after 'em.'

Slaughter allowed the stallion a brief drink of water and a sugar lump while Snipe roped a mustang from the remuda and set his own free. A sobbing woman, hauling a battered suitcase, was coming from the house and setting off on foot on the long dusty trail. Beneath her black shawl he recognized the grief-strained face of the duenna. 'After all I have done for them,' she wailed. 'I didn't know. . . .'

He ascertained from her what had gone on. 'Too bad,' he said, almost feeling sorry for her as she tottered away towards Visalia.

Aaron was saddling the new mustang and slung the saddle-bags behind. 'See what I boughtcha in town.' He opened one and produced five sticks of dynamite, waggling them at him. 'Might come in handy.'

'Thanks, Aaron.' Slaughter caught them as Snipe tossed them one by one to him; he put them in his pocket. 'Good thinking.'

He figured that Henry, in the prime of life, was good for another thirty miles. 'I ain't leaving this ol' boy behind. Come on, let's ride.'

Rancher Henderson had been making some preparations, too. He had purchased a shiny new Gatling gun, the 1875 model issued to small army garrisons in Indian country. He had mounted it on the roof of his adobe ranch house, its thick muzzle jutting out through the battlements, pointed at the flat expanse of prairie before it.

Suddenly, late afternoon, Raquel come skittering into the yard and almost fell from the horse, sobbing into his arms. Immaculately turned out, as always, Henderson patted her on the back, trying to prevent her tears from wetting his clean linen.

'Control yourself, Raquel,' he said. 'What's happened?'

Oh, Jack, my father's coming here to kill you. I'm sure of it.'

'Let him try,' the rancher snapped, breaking away from her clutching fingers. He went across to the bunkhouse to rouse those hands who weren't already on duty. He had also taken the precaution of recruiting from outlying towns more hardened gunslingers and now had a force of another ten well-armed men lined up before him. He began deploying them to various positions: the barn roof, the wagon shed, the bakery.

'The greasers are about to attack. They won't have a chance. There'll be a bonus to all of you boys at the end of the day. Come on, the rest of you. Up on the roof.'

Raquel had sunk into the dust, her riding-skirt spread around her, tears streaking her face powder, her blonde hair bedraggled. 'Oh, Jack,' she wailed. 'Don't you care about me? Why did you attack us?'

'Get into the house. And shut up. I cain't stand a snivelling woman.' He turned on his heel, calling back, 'Bolt the doors after you.'

Then he climbed to the roof and strode across to the Gatling gun. 'I've been itching to give this first blood,' he muttered. He adjusted its tripod to a comfortable height and squinted along the sights. He clacked in a box magazine of .45-70 cartridges, which would be gravity-fed into the bronze breech housing. He pulled the trigger and gave it a quick burst. He gave a smile of satisfaction. 'Old Don Miguel ain't gonna know what's hit him.'

He saw a cloud of dust on the horizon. 'Get ready, men,' he shouted. 'Here they come. Show no mercy.'

Everything was happening at once. Horses were going down, screaming their terror, hoofs kicking, eyes bulging, their bodies spouting blood. The riders were throwing up their hands in wild agony as the bullets from the stuttering Gatling hit them with bone-shattering impact, rolling them into the dust.

How could it be? Don Miguel wondered. They were 1,000 feet away from the ranch house. What was this new weapon of mass destruction, which he had never encountered before? Miraculously, he and Ricardo and a lucky few were unscathed by the hail of lead. They rode on, through the carnage, closer to the house, chased by a line of slugs spurting into the dust.

On his castellated roof Henderson laughed maniacally as he watched the *vaqueros* suffer. Hit 'em for six, boys,' he shouted to his men, who were picking off others of the invaders down below. 'A hundred dollars to whoever gets Don Miguel.'

'That'll be mine,' Hans Groper shouted, raising his carbine and spinning another Mexican from the saddle. 'It's like potting ducks on a pond. Where's he gotten to?'

'How dare they attack me?' Henderson screamed. 'This will teach them. I want no survivors. That's an order.'

He tossed an empty magazine away, reached for another, fitted it and returned to the attack.

Rat-a-tat-a-tat . . . Slaughter heard the machine gun rattling out as he and Aaron reached the scene, saw the horses and *vaqueros* going down in a balletic choreography of death.

'Christ!' he shouted. 'They've rode straight into it.'

He charged on in to join those who had escaped, who were riding in circles, confused by the attack.

'Get round the sides and the back,' he shouted in Spanish. 'Hey, *hombres*, it's no use charging straight in.'

'Agh!' gasped another *vaquero* as his spine was shattered by a bullet. Slaughter spotted the sniper on the bakery roof, raised his Spencer to his shoulder and took him out. The man dropped writhing in the dust.

'Watch out! There's more there, and there.' He pointed to the saddlery and stable roofs. 'Get them, *amigos*.'

Maybe he felt a kinship with these downtrodden Mexicans after two years of fighting for Benito Juárez.

Maybe he shared their atavistic approach to battle. Now, like them, his blood lust was provoked. It was kill or be killed.

Like all close-quarter forays with the enemy everything relied on split-second reaction. He rode his horse, leaping through the pandemonium, holding the reins in his teeth, guiding him with his knees and the sway of his body, pulling the Spencer tight to his shoulder, levering it and firing again and again until his bullets were gone. He stuffed the carbine back into the saddle boot, swung the stallion round, and drew his Schofield.

No time now for all that army bull of choosing a target, taking first pressure to make sure. No, it was a mindless, mad battle, blazing away, firing from the hip like lightning, for he who hesitates is lost.

Bodies of the Anglos were tumbling from their hiding-places, the Mexicans dispatching them point blank with their rifles, or leaping from their mustangs to disembowel them with machetes. The Gatling gun had started stuttering again, raking across the forecourt. But most of the Mexicans had moved in close to the house to escape its lead, firing up at any man on the battlements who dared show himself.

Slaughter pulled a stick of dynamite from his pocket and hurled it on to the house roof. Its explosion upon impact with a hard surface fountained debris, dust and assorted blood-dripping, spinning arms and legs and heads that splattered to the ground.

He rode on round the side of the house to a corner, and tossed two more sticks, causing a section of the roof to go crashing down upon poor Raquel who cowered inside directly below, although he did not know that, or care by now.

His killing streak aroused, Slaughter holstered his Schofield, stood up on the saddle and leapt for the battlements, hauling himself up and over. The dynamite had done its work and the rooftop was a scene of chaos. Through the smoke and dust, across a gaping hole in the roof, he saw Henderson twisting the Gatling around on its tripod to aim its nozzle at him. Henderson grinned, jerking at the trigger, but then cursed as the mechanism jammed.

Slaughter whipped out his Schofield but the rancher, in his black clothes, realizing that all was lost, was raising his hands. Slaughter aimed his revolver at him, but as he did so a bullet seared his cheek from close by. Turning, he saw Groper emerge from the smoke, both of his twin six-guns spitting lead.

Off balance, Slaughter rolled aside, and returned fire. His shot smashed into Hans Groper's knee, cutting him down. When Slaughter got to his feet and pointed his revolver at him the rustler was screaming.

'No, please, I saved your life. I shot that deputy. Don't kill me.'

'Yeah, framed me as a back-shooter, you mean,' Slaughter gritted out, but he hesitated, never one to kill an unarmed man.

A Mexican who leaped over the battlements to join him had no such fussiness. He stabbed a knife into Groper's jugular, making blood spout.

'I surrender,' Henderson shouted, as the bounty hunter returned his attention to him. 'You can have everything. Just give me a horse and I'll go. I'll leave the state. You'll never hear of me again.'

'Hmm?' Slaughter walked warily around to join him. 'That ain't exactly up to me.'

'Listen, man,' Henderson shouted. 'I'm offering you twenty-five thousand dollars to give me safe passage out of here.'

Slaughter pulled open a trapdoor which revealed some steep stairs down into the house. 'The only place I'm taking you is to jail. Lead on. It's over for you, pal. So you better show me where the cash is.'

'Not unless you promise to get me out of here.'

Slaughter shoved him. 'Get going.'

Raquel was dragging herself out of a pile of earth and debris in what had been Henderson's study, clawing the muck from her hair.

'You look a mess,' said Slaughter, grinning. 'Guess you wish you hadn't gotten into this now. Here's your boyfriend to see ya. You wanna give him a goodbye kiss?'

Raquel scowled at him and Henderson ignored her as he brushed dust from his immaculate black frock-coat.

'Where's the cash from the robbery?' Slaughter demanded. 'I know you were in it, both of you, and Ricardo. So you'd better start talking.'

'You know my terms,' Henderson insisted.

'Aw, I ain't got time to argue. Maybe it's in the safe.' Slaughter took a step back, taking his last stick of dynamite from his pocket. 'You better take cover,' he warned. He followed them back out of the room then threw the dynamite hard at the safe door, jumping back as the study went up in smoke. When it had cleared he found the safe door hanging from its hinges.

'Well, whadda ya know?' Slaughter marvelled as he lifted out wads of greenbacks. 'All the numbers tally. Looks like we've reached the end of the rainbow.'

When Aaron joined him Slaughter told him, 'You better go get your saddle-bags and get this li'l lot tucked away.'

When Snipe returned he said, 'Don Miguel wants Henderson outside.' He gave a whoop as he examined the hoard of dollars. 'Looks like we cracked it, James.'

'Yeah, seems so,' Slaughter agreed. 'Come on, Jack. You got some explainin' to do to your galfriend's father.'

'Be a white man,' Henderson pleaded. 'Help me.'

'A white man, huh? Hey, that's a laugh. Move it. Fast, you snivellin' coward. You're the one who started all this. Better men than you might still be alive . . . aw, come on.'

At the front of the house, as his remaining men taunted the wounded before dispatching them, taking what spoils of war they could gather, Don Miguel sat his horse, his dark face pensive beneath his sombrero.

'Henderson's my prisoner,' Slaughter shouted. 'In this country he's got the legal right to representation. As a law enforcer I'm taking him in.'

'Oh, *sí.*' Don Miguel agreed. 'I always wish to abide by the law. So, this is the rat who seduced my daughter?'

'Waal, it takes two to tango but, yeah, like I said, I'm taking him into Visalia.'

'I don' think so.' Ricardo had stepped across behind him and now stuck his ruby-studded revolver into Slaughter's back. 'That's not a good idea.' He slid the Schofield out of its holster and tossed it into the dust.

'My father makes the law in these parts.'

Henderson saw the grim look on Don Miguel's face and tried to break away, but two *vaqueros* stepped in to hold him.

The old man raised his shotgun and pointed it at Henderson's groin, poking it in close up. He squeezed both triggers. The explosions shattered flesh, bone and testicles and Henderson screamed, rolling in the dust.

'He won't be seducing any more girls.' Don Miguel turned his horse and headed back to his ranch. 'Tell my daughter she is welcome to him. She is on her own. She has no home with me.'

Slaughter stared at the screaming man, but was suddenly bludgeoned across the back of the neck. That was the last he remembered as darkness closed over him.

Ricardo smiled and stepped to the side of the door as Snipe ran out, saddle-bags over his shoulder, to see what was going on. 'Loo-tenant,' he cried. But he too received the same treatment.

'You men can go with my father,' said Ricardo. 'I will clear things up here. Take our dead with you.' He stepped across to Henderson and pressed his revolver to his head. 'Sorry, Jack. I can't stand this caterwauling.' He blew the rancher's skull apart.

'No!' Raquel screamed as she came out on to the porch and stared at her dead decapitated lover. 'Why?' She caught hold of Ricardo's arm. 'We could have shared the money between us.'

'Get off me.' He brushed her away, picked up the saddle-bags and watched the *vaqueros* trail away. 'Get my lariat. I have to rope these two.'

When he had Slaughter and Snipe tied he muttered, 'They deserve to die. But I feel I had better not kill two federal men.' He threw the saddle-bags over his mare's neck and swung into the saddle. 'Now it is time for me to disappear, go East and enjoy myself.'

'Take me with you,' Raquel hissed, hanging on to his leg in the stirrup. 'Please. Half of that money should be mine. Don't leave me.'

'So long, sis, as the *Americanos* say.' He spurred the mare away and, as Raquel tried to hang on to him, screaming, he kicked her sprawling in the dust. 'Have fun.'

TWELVE

'When's the next train north to Stockton?' Ricardo yelled through the grille of Visalia railroad office.

'Not until the morning,' the clerk replied. 'North at ten a.m. South at eight.'

'Hell.' The young Mexican frowned with disappointment. He had no wish to *ride* horseback the 150 miles. He had heard there was a Pullman car that went all the way to the east coast from Stockton. He had been planning on hanging out in the Mid-West, changing money in whatever towns he came to, then moving on. 'I should have killed those two.'

He leaped back on his mare and rode into town to the Devil's Cauldron. It was locked and shuttered. So he hitched the mare outside the Welcome Stranger. For the first time he felt uneasy about leaving the expensive horse and the gold-adorned saddle outside. But he arrogantly tipped his sombrero to hang on his back and pushed through the batwing doors. Heads swivelled to give the once-over at the flashy Mexican dude, his golden spurs clinking as he strode to the bar, his ruby-studded revolver on his hip.

In fact, Ricardo felt as nervous as a bobcat and twice as twitchy as he called for a beer. Maybe it had been foolish to spend the stolen gold coins so wantonly. Now he needed to change one of the bills. When the beer was slid to him he drank it back in one draw and offered a fifty note.

'Ain't you got anything smaller?' The 'keep examined the crisp new bill suspiciously, then went to compare it with serial numbers scrawled on a piece of cardboard behind the till. 'Where'd you get this?' he asked.

'Just give me the change.'

'I can't do that.' The 'keep called to a fellow barman, 'Hal, go get the deputy.'

'I wouldn't do that.' Ricardo pulled out his revolver, covering them. 'Give me that back.' He snatched the bill from the 'keep and backed out of the saloon.

Panic in him, he raced the mare out of town, quirting her from side to side, and headed up into the hills, making for the dark ridge of redwoods as darkness fell. Nobody would find him in the great sequoia forest. He would make his way south to Bakersfield and on to the border. 'I'll be safer in Old Mexico,' he whispered to himself.

When he regained consciousness Slaughter found himself hogtied so tight, a noose around his neck, tautly connected back to bind his wrists to his ankles that he was losing circulation in his hands and legs. Snipe, near by, was similarly bound.

'Jeez, where am I?'

'Where ya think you are?' Slaughter growled. 'On the porch of the Tarantula ranch.'

'Aw,' Aaron groaned. 'Somebody must have slugged me. They coulda cracked my skull.'

'You don't say? A fine mess you've got us into, Corporal. Thought you were s'posed to watch my back.'

'The sight of all that cash musta gone to my head.'

'Yeah, and Ricardo's, too. He'll be miles away with it by now.'

'He sure had you fooled, Loo-tenant.'

'Yuh, I must admit I didn't figure Ricky for a lousy crook at first. Guess he's shown his true colours.'

'Where is everybody?'

'Dead or departed.'

'What's happened to the gal?'

'Guess she's gone, too.'

'What, both of 'em? And taken the cash?'

'Guess so. They're hardly likely to have left it behind. I bet they're having a good old laugh about us.'

Slaughter craned his head to look around in the dusk at the carnage of bodies, men and horses, littering the yard. 'They made one mistake. They left us with our spurs on.'

'Oh, yuh.' Snipe held his legs tensed until Slaughter could wriggle his body down against his friend's boots and begin rubbing the bonds on his wrists against his spurs. 'Keep at it.'

'Ouch!' The sharp spur jagged Slaughter's wrist. It was impossible to see what he was doing and difficult to make purchase, but he persisted and was rewarded as gradually the rawhide lariat frayed and snapped.

'I'm loose,' he gasped. He sat and waggled his hands. 'Shee-it! I hardly got any feeling left.'

When Slaughter got blood back in his fingers he untied Snipe. 'Where'd he toss my Schofield?' he muttered. He searched around in the dust. 'Ah, here 'tis.'

'How long we been out?' Snipe hopped about, slapping at his legs, clapping his hands. 'Is it evening or dawn?'

'Whadda ya think? The sun's just gone down in the west. You sure ask some stoopid questions. Find yourself some guns and a hoss. There's plenty around. We gotta git movin'.' Slaughter put fingers to his mouth and gave a shrill whistle. 'Where's that crazy horse?'

When Henry came trotting through the gloaming he said, 'I'll give him a handful of corn over in the stables.'

As Slaughter led Henry away there was a flash of an explosion from a window of the house. A bullet whined past his head and smashed into the woodwork of the stable door.

Snipe, close to the porch, saw a shadowy movement behind a curtain. A rifle barrel poked through and Snipe heard the crash of another shot as the lieutenant ducked for cover. Snipe fired the revolver he had just picked up, following that up with three more fast shots.

'Got him!' he cried triumphantly.

But when Aaron went inside to investigate he changed his tune. 'Oh, holy Jasus,' he moaned with horror. 'What have I done?'

Raquel was lying there, blood oozing from a hole in her shoulder, fear in her blue eyes.

'I don't want to die,' she whimpered.

141

'Maybe you shoulda thought of that,' Slaughter said, as he joined them, ' 'fore you tried to kill us.'

'You started all this. If you hadn't come here we would have—'

'No, that rat Henderson started all this. And you and Ricky and Franco. Three good men died in that robbery because of your greed. And a lot more have gone to t'other side since he attacked your ranch. Can't you get that in your thick head?'

'Ah!' She wailed at the sight of her crimson blood. 'Help me.'

'We're trying to.' He tore her dress away, examined her front and back. 'Aaron, find some of Henderson's clean shirts. There must be some around. We need to plug this hole and truss her up.'

'Am I going to die?' She sounded like a frightened child, not the haughty beauty she had been.

'The slug's gone straight through. If there ain't no bits left in to pizen the blood you got a fifty-fifty chance. At least you won't have to face the surgeon's knife.'

When she was bandaged he told Aaron to ride to Don Miguel. 'Explain what happened. Tell him to bring that coach here to take her home.'

'But he's likely to shotgun me.'

'No, I don't think he'll do that.'

'Don't leave me,' Raquel moaned.

'I ain't a benevolent society. I'm going after that cash 'fore it's too late. There's bounty on you an' we oughta arrest you. But we're crossing you off our list. Why waste a good woman on the scaffold? Or a bad'un, come to that?'

'Thank you.' She made the sign of the cross over

142

herself. 'I've seen the light. I'm going to be good. I promise you that. I'll never sin again.'

'Yeah?' He squeezed her hand. 'Waal, I wouldn't overdo it.'

He went out, found his stallion, swung on board, and headed towards Visalia at a fast lope.

If he could follow the Rio Tulare up through the forest to its headwaters, cross the mountains and reach the North Fork of the River Kern, he would be able to make his way down to Bakersfield and head for the border.

At least, that was Ricardo's plan. But darkness had fallen fast and he was relieved to see the lights of the base logging camp. Some sort of dance was in progress, young couples heeling and toeing it on a wide redwood stump that made a good floor. A fiddle and banjo, the cries of delight, set the night alight.

They were mostly married couples, with babes, who lived in these cabins down here. The young women and girls were surprisingly good-looking in their modest, ankle-length dresses, and their men were sturdy honest types. They welcomed Ricardo to their feast, gave him food and drink, and as he watched their celebration it occurred to him that maybe not all Anglos were so bad. However, up in the back country where the single loggers worked it might be a different tale.

Slaughter hoved in among the throng in the Welcome Stranger and shouted across the bar, 'Gimme a whiskey.'

A farmer and a railroad linesman were loudly disputing beside him. 'Them telegraph wires of yourn burn my wheat,' the farmer cried. 'And I don't want folk down in Bakersfield hearing everything I'm sayin' to my wife.'

Slaughter caught the linesman's eye. 'Jeez, ain't there some nincompoops about,' he muttered, and then raised his own voice to roar, 'Hey, anybody seen that flashy Mex kid, Ricardo Puyol, around?'

'Yeah,' the farmer replied. 'I seen him as I was coming in. He was heading towards the Tulare river.'

'Right.' Slaughter took a sup of the whiskey. It was too dark to go after the Mexican now. He needed to rest his horse, and himself, come to that. It had been a busy day.

'That's him.' Hilarius Bogbinder had come into the saloon accompanied by the remaining deputy, Ernie Higgs. 'Arrest him,' the lawyer screamed. 'He broke into my office, stole my cash.'

'What you got to say, mister?' Higgs asked nervously.

'I'd say he's a twistin' li'l creep. There was no cash in that safe to steal, was there, Mr Bogsniffer?'

'He's lying. Do your duty, go on!' The lawyer tried to push the deputy forward as Slaughter calmly put his glass aside.

'I ain't got time to argue with cheatin', crawlin' snakes like you,' drawled Slaughter. He stepped forward, hoisted the screeching lawyer up by his cravat, grabbed a leg and hurled him over the bar to smash against the mirror and bottles and crash to the floor. 'So long.' He dusted his hands as if at a good job done, turned to the deputy. 'You got anything to say?'

Ernie made a face and shrugged. 'I didn't see nuthin'.'

'Did anybody else see me touch Mr Bagbinder?'

144

Slaughter asked as the lawyer crawled out from behind
the bar.

'Nah,' the linesman guffawed. 'We didn't see nuthin',
did we boys?'

'Good.' Slaughter flipped one of the late sheriff's
twenty-dollar bills on to the bar. 'Give 'em all a whiskey.'

He walked out, collected his stallion and took him
along to the livery. Time to snatch a few hours shut-eye
in the straw.

Steam-powered circular saws buzzed and whined as in
the early dawn Ricardo left the base camp. The men
there would cut through many thousands of board-feet a
day.

Soon they were left far behind and he entered the
great cathedral of sequoias, soaring 300 feet into the sky.
There was a brooding silence, his surroundings were on
a scale that made mere man seem Lilliputian. They were
the tallest living things on earth. The young Mexican
stared upwards, awestruck. He had heard that some were
so wide at the base that rooms had been hollowed into
their huge butts.

At first the going was easy but when he reached the
fast-flowing river tumbling down from the 4,500-foot
peaks of the Sierra Nevada the banks were so steep and
rocky that he was forced to move back into the trees.

Suddenly he came across a scene of wholesale destruction where lumbermen had ravaged the groves and were
still busy doing so. A swath of fallen giants, most about
700 years old, lay all about as workmen sawed them into
logs and rolled them with crowbars down a bank on to

sturdy wagons drawn by teams of twenty yoked oxen, to be dragged away to the base camp and, when sliced, on to the railroad.

Two men, precariously balanced ten feet up on spring-boards, were laying into another huge redwood with a long whipsaw. There was a cracking sound as the tree's branches interlocked with others and the whipboarders jumped for their lives as the redwood kicked back, the earth trembling as it fell.

Ricardo made his way around the scene. There was no point in trying to head through the dense virgin forest so he followed a trail up the steep mountainside. It was so treacherous that he had to dismount and walk. Soon he was bitterly regretting his decision to try to get through this way.

Greased pine logs had been laid as a kind of tramway down which plodding oxen, urged on by their cursing whacker, dragged toboggans on to which vast tree trunks were chained. Ricardo was forced off the trail as they passed.

So the day wore on. Ricardo, dragging his mare, became exhausted and hungry, feeling thoroughly out of his element. This world was a far cry from the rolling plains where he used to ride like a lord of all he surveyed, protected by his *vaquero* band. His fancy, high-heeled boots weren't made for walking. But he had to persevere. There was no going back now.

By nightfall he had begun to dread sleeping out in these sinister woods where grizzlies prowled. So he was glad at first, to reach one of the back-country camps. It was a lopsided collection of rickety cabins with shingle roofs.

146

The narrow street was littered with empty barrels and logs.

Red Dog Hotel – Beds – Licker – Eats, announced the painted sign over the doorway of a two-storey joint. Six bearskins had been nailed to a wall to cure, and a bunch of scruffy men, hunters with guns in their hands, lounged on barrels outside and eyed the young *vaquero* with sullen curiousity.

'Hi!' A curly-haired young woman hung out of a bedroom window. 'Come inside.'

Ricardo decided to accept the invitation, so he hitched the mare near by, hauled off his expensive saddle and the saddle-bags stuffed with greenbacks, swung them over his shoulder and staggered inside. He dumped the heavy rig in a dark, dingy bar as the girl came clattering down the stairs to join him. She was in a revealing blouse and bell-shaped skirt. She caught hold of his arm and said, 'I'm Ruby. Who are you? Let's sit over here.' She drew him to a corner bench, hugging herself into him.

Ricardo reluctantly introduced himself and stuffed the sadde-bags under the bench.

'What do you do, Ruby?' he asked. 'Do you work here?'

'No, I'm a guest. I sell ladies' magazines.' She giggled, suggestively. 'Some of the pictures are a little risqué. The men seem to like them. Where are you going, Ricky? What's a handsome *vaquero* like you doing up here?'

'I'm tryin' to get through to the North Fork river. Where's this trail lead to?'

'Nowhere. It's just a sheer cliff face at the back of here.'

147

'So, why is this hotel here?'

'It's where the lumberjacks come to for a little randy and rowdy entertainment. They're mighty rough, those boys. But don't worry, that's only paydays. It's quiet tonight. Just you and me.'

'What about those men outside?'

'Aw, them. They're fine, but they're spent up. They ain't got a dime 'tween 'em now.' Her fingers were roaming all over him. 'I cain't wait to git acquainted. You wanna come up and see my magazines?'

'I'm hungry. I need to eat.' Apart from the stink of a fish-oil lamp, there was a ripe odour emanating from a pot on an iron stove. 'What have they got?'

'Help yourself, *señor*. There's a bit of everything in here.' A muscular-chested man in a roll-neck jersey, his pants held up by thick suspenders over his shoulders, a derby perched on his head, had come from a back room, and gave the pot a stir. 'Or howabout a fresh grizzly steak?'

Ricardo sniffed the tangy aroma. 'I'll try a bit of this.'

The bar-owner, whose hair was as tight and curly as Ruby's tangled mop, grinned and ladled him some into a wooden bowl. 'How about something to put hairs on your chest?'

'*Sí*, OK. But I have a difficulty. I only have a fifty. Can you give me change?'

'A fifty, huh?' The barman examined it against the lamplight. 'Sure, no trouble.' He tucked it in his pocket. 'You enjoy yourself.'

When he turned around Ricardo saw Ruby down on one knee poking under the bench, into his saddle-bags.

'Hey, don't do that,' he called sharply. 'Keep out of there.'

'I was only looking to see if you'd got any cigarettes,' She pouted and cuddled back up to him as he sat down. 'Why are you so unfriendly?'

'Don't take no notice of Ruby. She's a nosy little tyke.' The barman introduced himself as Mike and slammed a pot of liquor before him. 'Have a taste of that.'

'Whew!' The whiskey kicked through him, warming his blood. 'Firewater.'

'Yeah.' Mike, with his big, clean-shaven chin, looked a bit of a bruiser and topped him up with whiskey, splashing some in his soup. 'This is the beginnng of a great love affair.'

'Yes, with me, too, I hope.' Ruby's fingers stroked his thigh as he ate, then hovered over the grip of his pistol. 'Wow! Look at this. Are these real rubies? They're named after me.'

'Don't touch it.' He gulped, catching her hand. 'It's got a hair trigger. A sneeze could set it off. Just calm down, will you!'

But Ruby was like a cat on heat, climbing over him to look at his saddle. 'The man with the golden horn,' she gasped, gazing up at him. 'Mister, you've got it all.'

'Yes, and I intend to hang on to it.' He pushed the bowl away, cursing himself silently for being such a dumb fool. Why had he parted with that note? He needed to extricate himself from this sticky situation. 'That was very nice. I've got to be moving on.'

'Moving on?' Suddenly Ruby's dark eyes looked as deadly as a snake's. 'Where the hell you think you're moving to? There ain't no place to go.'

'What's wrong?' Mike demanded, coming back into the room followed by three of the men from outside. 'You want a steak or not?'

'No.' Ricardo tried to get to his feet but his head seemed to spin. 'I'm leaving. Just give me my change.'

'Change?' Mike grinned, smacking a billy stick on his palm. 'What change?'

In spite of his haste Slaughter had to pause to admire the nerve of a high-climber 200 feet up topping a tree, twanging back and forth as it fell, or marvel at the skill of peelers hacking back the redwood's foot-thick bark. Other men were clearing water flumes that enabled logs to go speeding down the slopes at fifty miles an hour.

It was hard, dangerous work, worse in winter. Death was no stranger in these woods. Like cowboys, most loggers were nomads with no ties, constantly moving on, with a penchant for booze, brawls and bawds.

The mass immigration to the West had created a soaring demand for housebuilding wood and the loggers were there to feed it and a worldwide market. But they were lucky to make a dollar a day. The profits went into the pockets of the timber millionaires.

'Seen any sign of a Mexican?' he called out as he climbed the slope. He was pointed on his way.

As a boy he had educated himself by leafing through a big old encyclopaedia, so he knew that the sequoia had been named after the Cherokee chief Secqoyah, who had devised an alphabet for his tribe. Such useless knowledge filled his head!

150

Night fell suddenly and it was all but pitch dark when he reached a Y-fork in the trail. In the flicker of his matches he read a sign. Dollarhide Camp to the right. Red Dog t'other way. Maybe he should toss a coin? His stallion decided for him, scenting the air and setting off for Red Dog.

A bunch of men were barbecueing bear steaks over a blazing fire. Beyond was a clapboard hotel. Henry was in a state of great excitement, for the mare was hitched outside and, whinnied a greeting.

Suddenly Slaughter heard a female scream, a shot and shouts and noise coming from the hotel.

'You behave,' he told Henry. He hitched the horse tight to a forked log and went to investigate.

Inside the Red Dog Ruby had sneaked Ricardo's revolver out of his holster as he stood to argue with Mike. He gave her a backhander across the jaw as he tried to snatch it back. It exploded as Mike's shillelagh cracked down across the back of his neck. Already dazed by the liquor Ricardo desperately fought back. But three burly loggers had joined in the fray, smashing his nose, pounding his ribs, knocking him to the floor.

Another of the 'hunter-loggers' had his shotgun primed. As Slaughter burst in the thug fired at him. The lead pellets peppered the ceiling as the Spencer's bullets' bone-crushing impact hurled him back against the wall.

The loggers stopped stomping on Ricardo with caulked boots and turned their attentions to Slaughter. Ruby was waggling the revolver at him, so, instinctively he aimed his fifth bullet at her wrist. She howled and

151

dropped the gun as if it was red hot.

Mike's club swung hard, knocking the Spencer from Slaughter's hands. After that all he knew was flying fists thudding into him as he parried haymakers, dodged spiked boots, and flung a brute from his back who was gnawing at his ear. It was the toughest bareknuckle bout he'd ever been in. He jabbed two fingers in the eyes of Mike to stop him, headbutted another, kicked a third attacker in the goin, and swapped seemingly endless blows with yet another who was as big and hairy as a bear. But it was a fight for life or death and he eventually sent them tumbling and crawling away.

'Hell!' He stood panting, blood trickling from his chewed ear. 'You guys certainly like a scrap.'

The husky bear was getting to his feet again so Slaughter picked up his Spencer and poleaxed him.

'Anybody else?' He glowered at them, retrieved Ricardo's fancy pistol and showered a concatenation of bullets from it over their heads, smashing mugs and bottles. The racket made them cringe.

'This ain't fair,' Ruby wailed, nursing her torn wrist. 'Where'd *you* come from?'

'I'm a Pinkerton man,' Slaughter shouted, as the loggers from outside arrived, peering through the gun-smoke and wreckage. 'This man's my prisoner, wanted for train robbery and homicide. I'm taking him outa here. If anybody interferes I warn you from now on, I'm shooting to kill.'

The loggers seemed at first bemused, gawping at the scene, then cackling at Mike and his pals' discomfiture, and, in fact, helping the bloody Ricardo to his feet. They

152

lugged out his expensive saddle while Slaughter made sure of the saddle-bags.

'Aw, no,' he groaned, as he limped outside. 'That's all I need.'

The stallion had dragged his log down the street and was up on his hind legs busy serving the mare, as they say. This made the men cheer and laugh some more as they waited to help saddle them.

'You're in a mess, aincha, boy?' Slaughter tucked Ricardo's revolver into his own belt and examined him. 'Broken nose. Fractured ribs. Broken finger. And those spiked boots ain't done much fer ya looks. Serves you right, all the trouble you've caused.'

'Why not string him up now,' a logger suggested. 'We like a good hanging.'

'Nah, I believe in lawful process,' Slaughter said, 'an' I need the bounty on him.'

However, they insisted he enjoy a bear steak and a bite of the bottle before sending him on his way. 'Moon's fit to rise. Should be easier downhill.'

'What do you think I'll get?' Ricky groaned as he hung on to his golden horn.

'If they don't hang ya, about fifteen years' hard labour. With good behaviour you'll be out in ten. You'll still be a young man. Waal, sorta. Don't fret, *amigo*, there's a nice cosy cell waiting for you in Visalia.'

THIRTEEN

'Huccome you call your horse Henry?' Aaron asked, as they sat on a bench at the railroad station having just missed the south bound 8 a.m. train.

'There was this drunken newspaper man used to hang around in Tooh-sohn,' Slaughter drawled. 'He wrote dime Westerns as a sideline. Allus slinging questions at me about bounty hunting. How many had I killed? How did they attack me? Henry Remington was his handle. He looked like a horse. Hence, Henry—'

The roar of the locomotive rushing in, the press of folks hurrying to get on, drowned any other words. Doc Dixon was among the passengers, standing at a window talking to his daughter, Kathleen. She waved goodbye as the ten a.m. northbound pulled out, woodsmoke blasting its column into a clear blue sky.

Kathleen's neatly brushed hair was tinged with grey. Her respectable dress and cardigan were grey, too, clinging to her slim, shapely figure as she turned to go.

'Good morning,' she greeted Slaughter. 'Dad's off to a judges' conference in San Francisco for a couple of

154

days. He spotted you and asked me to tell you that Mr Bogbinder will be disbarred on account of his illegal activities, from practising law in the whole of California. I would like to thank you. I feel as if I can breathe again, freed from their constant threats.'

'Good to hear it.' Slaughter grinned and indicated the bench. 'Why don't you jine us? Or you in a hurry to go?'

'No.' She glanced around, a little flustered, but most people had gone. 'I've dropped the children in school. They won't be home 'til four. I've nothing else to do all day.'

'I better be on my way.' Aaron nudged Slaughter and jumped to his feet. 'I gotta see Elspeth. We're thinking of opening a pharmacy store. There's good money in it.'

'OK. If you change your mind I'll be catching the six o'clock south tonight.' Slaughter watched Aaron go, put his arm up on the back of the bench and faced Kathleen. 'Elspeth is his lady love.'

'So I gathered. You're not going to sit here all day waiting for your train are you?'

'Why? Can you think of better things to do?' He met her grey-green eyes. 'You're a war widow, aincha?'

'Yes, but my husband fought on the opposite side to you.'

'War was a long time ago. Aincha thought of gettin' hitched again?'

'No.' She lowered her eyes, studied her hands. 'I've never met a man to compare. How about you? Are you wed?'

'Nah. I was. She died.'

'Oh, I'm sorry, how did that happen?'

'I killed her.'

'What?'

'We married when she was fifteen.' He took a deep breath, for he had rarely spoken about it. 'After four years away in the war I went home. Found her in bed with a bluebelly officer. He went for his gun. I shot him. Then I put a bullet between her eyes.'

'Poor girl. She must have been lonely.'

'Yeah. That didn't occur to me at the time.' He slapped the Schofield. 'This is the gun I used. Every time I kill a man I think of her.'

'You are a very violent man, but I think, perhaps, a lonely one.'

'I'm sick of killing. I've had fourteen years of it. I just wanna relax.'

Her knee brushed his as she moved. Was it intentional? He glimpsed her ankle. Her stockings were grey, too. She seemed disturbed, wanting to leave, but reluctant to. He reached out and squeezed her hand. 'You know what I'd like to do today? Be with you.'

Kathleen nodded. 'I've never . . . not since. . . .'

'Yeah, well, it would be an oasis in the desert for me, too.'

'I must go.' She got to her feet, bit her lip, then turned back to him. 'I will tell Clarence to go visit his family for the day. Come round in a hour. You can leave your horse in the garden.'

She was all he expected her to be, shy and soft as he slowly undressed her on the bed and caressed and kissed her body.

'I've never done it like this,' she whispered. 'In the daylight, I mean. It was always in the dark under the bedclothes.'

Maybe he aroused her latent sexuality because gradually their lovemaking became real wild. Lonely women make the best lovers, or so they say. Maybe lonely men do, too.

Kathleen cooked him ham and eggs, served it in bed, and found a bottle of her father's brandy for him. 'Could you ever think about settling down around here?' she asked. 'There'll be a lot of land going for sale soon. Only three dollars an acre, too.'

'It's an attractive idea, but I'm a man of the wide open spaces. This state's a tad too civilized for my taste.' He winced as he touched the open cut on his cheek from Raquel's riding quirt. 'I guess I'd allus be an unwelcome stranger in this town.'

'So that's all we are to you?' There was a bitter tang to her tone. 'Just passing strangers? Surely, if you stayed, we could find some peace, some happiness?'

'I got a lot to do.' It was half past three and he began to pull on his clothes. 'You got your kids to collect. I got a train to catch. I want to get this twenty-five thousand dollars to the bank in Tucson. And get my share.'

There was a pained look in her eyes as she stood at the front door in her dressing-gown and they kissed.

'I'll think about it,' he said. 'About buying a ranch someplace. I'll write to you.'

He gave a whistle and when Henry galloped up he cinched him tight and swung into the saddle. He swirled him around and stood in the bentwood stirrups as the

157

stallion pawed the air. Slaughter gave the woman a wave. 'So long, Kathleen.'

Maybe I will come back, he thought, as he rode the horse away. Or is that just a crazy dream?

AUTHOR'S NOTE

This Western is based on a Pinkerton investigation of a similar train robbery in California at the time. The descriptions of life there in the mid-1870s are based on historical records. Otherwise, all characters and events are fictional. In 1882 the invention of the donkey engine meant that the use of bull teams and horse power in the woods would soon become a thing of the past. This engine and increased mechanisation enabled the forests to be ravaged with even greater intensity. However, in spite of corruption and bribery of Washington politicians by the timber companies, by the end of the century the conservation movement, backed by President Roosevelt, ensured that the mighty sequoia was saved. In 1890 the forest area in this story was made the USA's second national park.